OTHER FIVE STAR WESTERNS
BY T. T. FLYNN:

Night of the Comanche Moon (1995)
Rawhide (1996)
Long Journey to Deep Cañon (1997)
Death Marks Time in Trampas (1998)
The Devil's Lode (1999)
Ride to Glory (2000)
Prodigal of Death (2001)
Hell's Cañon (2002)
Reunion at Cottonwood Station (2003)
Outlaws (2004)
Noose of Fate (2005)
Dead Man's Gold (2006)
Gunsmoke (2007)
Last Waltz on Wild Horse (2008)
Shafter Range (2009)
A Bullet for the Utah Kid (2010)
Travis (2011)

THE RESURRECTION KID

THE RESURRECTION KID

A WESTERN QUARTET

T. T. FLYNN

FIVE STAR

A part of Gale, Cengage Learning

GALE
CENGAGE Learning·

Detroit • New York • San Francisco • New Haven, Conn • Waterville, Maine • London

GALE
CENGAGE Learning®

LIBRARY OF CONGRESS CATALOGING-IN-PUBLICATION DATA

Flynn, T. T.
    The resurrection kid : a Western quartet / by T.T. Flynn. — 1st
ed.
      p. cm.
    ISBN 978-1-4328-2610-9 (hardcover) — ISBN 1-4328-2610-7
(hardcover)
    I. Title.
PS3556.L93R47 2012
813'.54—dc23   2012015180

First Edition. First Printing: September 2012.
Published in conjunction with Golden West Literary Agency.
Find us on Facebook– https://www.facebook.com/FiveStarCengage
Visit our Web site– http://www.gale.cengage.com/fivestar/
Contact Five Star™ Publishing at FiveStar@cengage.com

Printed in Mexico
1 2 3 4 5 6 7 16 15 14 13 12

ADDITIONAL COPYRIGHT INFORMATION

CONTENTS

DEATH'S DEPUTY 9

DEATH TAKES A TALLY 45

KILLER COME HOME 107

A GUN FOR THE RESURRECTION KID 169

★ ★ ★ ★ ★

DEATH'S DEPUTY

★ ★ ★ ★ ★

Mike Tilden, who was the acquisitions editor at Popular Publications' Western pulp magazines, including *Dime Western*, often preferred to title each story he bought himself. When Ted Flynn knew beforehand where a story was going to be sent by his agent, as in this case, he titled it in the pay book he kept simply "Western." He finished this story on July 6, 1948. Mike Tilden bought it at thirty-eight typescript pages for $280.00 and titled it "Death's Deputy" upon publication in *Dime Western* (11/48).

I

Crimson twilight hung outside the train windows, glorifying the desert that Lon Hagerman had been watching steadily. It had been his desert once, in a way. He had lived near its edge and it had not changed.

The brakeman came through and lighted the brass lamps overhead. Night lunged down and presently the engine whistle screamed. The twangy-voiced conductor called in from the noisy platform: "*Allll* out for Bitter Wells!"

Hagerman stirred on the dusty red plush as the train jolted to a stop. He knew the cinder platform and weather-faded little depot. In days gone by he had stood out there under the wan platform lights, one of the station idlers watching trains come in.

Oily heat from the brass lamps came down on the crowd in the aisle. Many would change here at Bitter Wells to stage lines running into the back country. Hagerman thrust up the loose window and leaned toward the night's fresh coolness. He looked out for a familiar face, and for a second he sat like stone, his own long face dark and dangerous.

His hand went inside his dark blue coat to a bone-handled gun snugged under the left arm. This action required no thought. It occurred like the drive of a firing pin after the gun hammer has been tripped.

A black straw bonnet with yellow-dyed cock feathers appeared under the train window. The matronly woman under the bonnet paused on the platform, her faint smile of expectancy turned toward the train steps.

The big-chested man Hagerman was eyeing—a man all beef and muscular bulk below a powerful neck—passed the woman. His hand touched his hat.

Hagerman's thumb held rigid on the gun hammer with the muzzle poised just under the dusty window sill as the big-chested man moved on. His expression was that of a man who never forgot that someday, somewhere, he would confront the source of some really deep unease. Hagerman's mouth opened to call out sharply.

The plump woman and her bobbing yellow feathers moved a step, unconsciously shielding the powerful figure that walked on, unsuspecting. By so little as yellow rooster feathers across the line of sight was the matter decided. Hagerman returned the gun to the armpit holster.

Movement in the aisle drew the upraking glance of his brown, bitter eyes. He surprised a fascinated, frightened interest on a girl's face.

She had been leaving the coach, carrying a small valise. She had sighted the drawn gun and come to a startled stop. She moved on, a slight pallor on her lips, a quick flush appearing on her cheeks under Hagerman's raking stare. She was slim and sun-colored, with dark hair and a straight free grace in her passing.

Hagerman slowly pushed a handkerchief across his forehead. He stared absently at the train grime on the white cloth, not really seeing it because of the image of the girl. She had known what was happening. Perhaps she'd looked out and seen the big-chested man. At the very least she'd known what was in Hagerman's mind.

He stood up and pulled the scuffed cowhide suitcase from the rack overhead and turned into the aisle. The girl had already left the train. A huddle of passengers was ready to board as Hagerman crowded down the steps.

The lanky conductor said: "Not your stop, mister!"

"I'll try it," Hagerman said briefly, and walked on.

The yellow bonnet feathers were there ahead. Their owner was talking with the girl. Hagerman walked toward them, his long face impersonal and unconscious self-assurance in the wide set of his mouth.

He saw the girl only half listening as she sighted his approach. The tenseness was back about her, and some of the fascinated, almost frightened interest.

It struck Hagerman suddenly, disagreeably, that she could be dangerous. She was the one person in Bitter Wells who could guess why he'd stepped off the train.

He wondered if she'd told the older woman about the gun he'd drawn. Then a vagrant impulse hit him. He lifted the curved-brim gray Stetson as he came abreast of the two. He gave the girl a wickedly secret half smile, as if all things lay between them, and was not surprised at the startled disapproval on the older woman's face.

Annoyance touched the girl. So she had a temper. Hagerman's smile lingered as he walked on. Then the pair left his mind. He had not quitted the train to smile at strange women.

His raking look probed through the lighted station windows and did not find the big-chested man in there. His name, called in strident surprise that carried along the platform, brought him wheeling around.

"Lon Hagerman! By God! It's Lon Hagerman hisself!"

It would have happened later anyway. Hagerman smiled with genuine warmth as old Jiminy Jones came off a box beside the station door. They shook hands. A toothless grin split Jiminy's deep-wrinkled face. He had the timeless look of a mummy. Jiminy had looked like this when Hagerman was a boy. He'd be like this always, meeting the trains at Bitter Wells.

"Growed up real famous, didn't you, Lonnie?" Jiminy cackled. "We've heered plenty talk. I win ten dollars when word come you took the marshal's job at Silver Fork. 'They won't kill Lonnie there, neither,' I says. 'Look at the ones has been kilt already when they crowded Lon Hagerman's law badge! He's death,' I says. 'Death from Bitter Wells, by jiminy! An' 'twas old Jiminy Jones started him shootin' straight!' Remember?"

Hagerman said, smiling: "That's right, Jiminy. Mighty nice to see you. We'll have a drink tomorrow."

Old Jiminy Jones showed red gums in a happy grin. "We sure will! You home to stay now?"

"I'm looking around," Hagerman said, still smiling. "See you tomorrow, Jiminy."

He noted faces all along the platform gazing toward him with a new kind of wary interest. It always happened like this when his name was known. The neighborly indifference of passing strangers turned reserved, watchful. Respectful and a little fearful sometimes, and very often sullen, resentful. He was Lon Hagerman.

Long ago Hagerman had learned there was a price to everything. Being Lon Hagerman had its price. He saw that the slim girl was standing as if frozen, all her attitude changed. Such changes were part of the price, too. The price of being Lon Hagerman.

He could have guessed almost to a word what was running through her mind. Hagerman's smile was wry, regretful, as he rounded the end of the station in a loose, cautious prowl, suitcase in left hand, right hand easily near the open coat front. She had been a girl to remember.

He knew all eyes on the platform had followed him. Eyes would watch all his movements now as word spread through the town. That was part of the price, too. He'd known it would hap-

14

pen when he stepped off the train.

The brass engine bell began its impatient chiming. There was movement behind the station. Voices were audible at the horses, rigs, and buckboards tied there.

A rider wheeled out and touched his horse into a slow trot. Hagerman halted, peering at the shadowy figure as it passed close. Not his man.

He stood for a moment, looking toward the hitch rack, then went on into town, searching all movement in the night. Some of it was caution, so much a part of him now that most people never noticed. It took such caution to keep alive. That, too, was part of the price of being Lon Hagerman.

It was Saturday night, which accounted for the many idlers at the station. Hitch racks along Main Street were filled. A Saturday crowd of men, women, and children moved in and out of stores and along the walks.

Main Street was longer than Hagerman remembered, with many new buildings, more and larger saloons. But the town still stood beside the desert, with the formidable Maverick Mountains to the north and rough, dry range land south and east, and sweeter grass on the higher range to the north. All of it, desert and mountains and harsh range had marked the town.

Hagerman had become something of an expert in sizing up a town by the saloons and stir of life along Main Street. He missed nothing now, trying to see what Bitter Wells had become.

When a noisy group of cowhands spilled out of a saloon ahead and came toward him along the crowded plank walk, Hagerman stepped over against the building front with his suitcase and watched with steady intentness. He had sighted a man being elbowed carelessly aside by one of the group. They came his way now in a kind of jostling V, pointed by a thick, powerful young man with slouching shoulders and long arms.

Hagerman estimated the square aggressive face, strong-muscled jaws, low-lidded eyes under a carelessly slanted hat brim. The young man came on, grinning and tossing remarks over his shoulder, heedless of whom he elbowed and shouldered aside. The noisy group at his heels did the same.

The leader's elbow struck a woman's arm and her bundles spilled. He plowed on, not looking around.

Hagerman shook his head regretfully. It was no business of his. Yet this had been his town once and women had not been jostled on the walks.

He stepped out with the suitcase and the young man shouldered against him. Hagerman dropped the suitcase. The young man tripped over it, grabbing at Hagerman's arm, swearing in quick irritation.

Hagerman's straight-armed palm to the ribs sent the other reeling, tripping over his own crossed legs, down to hands and knees against the building front.

Laughter of the men behind chopped off into silence. They were seven, Hagerman counted with a swift glance. The ones at the rear weren't sure what had happened.

They bunched to a stop, filling the walk. All were armed. Several were wearing chaps. Most of them young and rough-looking. They had been drinking. They had been boisterous a moment ago. Now suddenly they were edgy, anticipating trouble as their leader came up grinning dangerously, letting his hat lay where it had fallen.

"Shoved me, didn't you, mister?" he demanded.

"One way of looking at it," Hagerman agreed. His back was to the walk edge, where he could watch them all. Movement had paused on the plank walk and in the street. This was trouble.

Hagerman had seen it happen more times than he liked to recall. He knew he was a fool, but he had lived in this town once. He had been a boy here, and he had had dreams. The thick-shouldered young stranger was measuring him. "I ain't seen you before. Stranger in this town?"

"It's changed since I saw it last," Hagerman told him mildly. "Women didn't get pushed around then. Most men didn't, either."

"You say I pushed you?"

"Apologize to the lady and move on. I don't want trouble," Hagerman said regretfully.

But he had trouble. It was there in the tight-lipped grin and bunching cheek muscles. This one could hold back, cat-and-mouse-like, savoring what he meant to do while the audience grew.

Then a voice called loudly, sarcastically from the street behind Hagerman. "You bit it off this time, Buck Lacy! That's Lon Hagerman! How does he chew?"

Hagerman had seen this happen, too. Had watched angry threat change to veiled dismay and a kind of inner harried withdrawal from furious intent.

Buck Lacy's query came in thick unbelief. "Are you Lon Hagerman?"

"None of your business," Hagerman told him, grateful to the man who had called out. He couldn't turn his head now and see who it was. He said patiently: "I don't want trouble. Just step back and apologize to the lady and move on."

Now there was more room around them. The quiet had a stunned, waiting quality. Buck Lacy licked his lips. His eyes had narrowed.

It was an old story to Hagerman. This Buck Lacy suddenly was wondering if he had a chance against Lon Hagerman. Wondering. Tempted. Fascinated by what it could mean to be the man who finally dropped Lon Hagerman. And against that he was balancing the figure he'd cut before the town if he took Hagerman's order.

Sometimes they tried. Hagerman's hands were loose at his

sides. The coat front was carelessly open. But it looked a long way to the gun under his left arm.

Buck Lacy's six-shooter was prominent in the holster against his leg. Near his hand. Ready. Hagerman almost sighed. Sometimes they tried. They kept trying.

"No trouble, Lacy," he repeated. "I know you didn't mean to spill the lady's packages. Looked to me like you might have been turning back to apologize when you bumped into me." Hagerman waited a moment and urged hopefully: "That's what happened, wasn't it?"

Often it worked. Offer a man a way that would leave him still a man, except down deep inside where he knew the truth, and trouble smoothed over.

Now and then a bully took it wrong and decided he wasn't the one trying to back out.

Buck Lacy's eyelids tightened down with a bit more tension and Hagerman knew regretfully what was coming. No relief there. Only tension, tightening for trouble.

Lacy smiled with his mouth corners down, faintly sneering, and said: "You saw everything, didn't you, mister?"

Hagerman agreed almost sadly: " 'Most everything, Lacy. 'Most everything."

He was standing patiently when Lacy turned the sneering smile to the silent bunch he had led along the walk. It brought Lacy's belt holster just right. When his hand slapped to the gun butt, it was fast.

But big Jutie Crane in Silver Fork had been faster. Dallas Red, in Cañon, had been faster on the draw. One-thumb Joe Brock, at Vega, had been far faster. And where were they? And others?

Hagerman had the helpless feeling that nothing ever changed. One day, of course, he'd be slow. Too slow. But not this time. Not this one.

He watched the gun fly out of Lacy's shattered hand, blasting futilely into the boardwalk as it spun down. The double pound of the shots, almost together, filled his ears once again as his gun covered Lacy's friends.

Hagerman didn't know it, but his face had again taken the tight-drawn, stony look. Hard. No mercy. It was the way he felt now. The way he had to feel, to live, once trouble broke.

"The lady now," Hagerman said. "Quick, Lacy. Quick, I tell you."

Not his voice, either, this cold grating order, strong enough to carry through a crowd. No mercy. Once they reached for a weapon, mercy meant death for him sooner or later. This way was why he was still Lon Hagerman. Why most men paused before they tried.

Buck Lacy stood stupefied. His eyes went down to the bloody hand in dull surprise, as if it were no part of him.

Then his glance jerked up to Hagerman's face and the fear hit him. He had clasped death. Its grip was on him. Lon Hagerman would decide behind that dark and dangerous face.

"Last chance!" said Hagerman harshly.

Buck Lacy shivered. His first step was unsteady. Then he moved in silence, the hand hanging at his side and blood dripping from the fingertips against his leg and spattering on his dusty riding boots.

His friends edged aside, letting him pass. They were a sullen, uncertain lot. Their guns could have downed Hagerman. They were thinking of it, Hagerman guessed from the shifty glances that slid his way.

But they knew the price. They made all this Buck Lacy's business alone, and let Lacy pass toward the woman while Hagerman's cold face watched above the cocked gun.

II

She was a gaunt, hard-worked woman off some small ranch. Her graying hair was caught in a neat bun at the back of her neck. She had the patient look of too many children, lean years, little money, and her reward in home and family held together.

She had picked up her dropped packages and stepped out past the hitch rack to a rickety buckboard. Her man would be in town somewhere, not knowing what had happened. She had dropped the packages in the buckboard while gunfire crashed nearby. Now she stood straight, rather fearfully by the front wheel as Lacy halted at the walk edge. A man coughed across the street. The sound was audible in the stillness.

Lacy's thick words were barely understandable. "Didn't mean to bump you, lady."

She opened her mouth. She swallowed, then wordless, she nodded.

"Good enough," said Hagerman shortly. "Now move on the way you were headed."

Lacy came slowly back, still too shocked to be sullen, and hesitated beside his gun.

"Pick it up by the barrel," Hagerman ordered.

Lacy did so, and stood, not turning his head, when Hagerman said: "I'll know you all next time. Think it over."

Lacy walked on then, his hand dripping blood and his gaze straight ahead. The others shuffled after him, knowing now about Lon Hagerman.

A red-faced man sidled out from the barbershop doorway a few steps away and blurted: "You made them VP boys beller low! Going to stay with us?"

"I'd pick a town where women aren't bothered," Hagerman said, and walked on with his suitcase.

Two riders were in the street. A buggy was just starting on. A buckboard was moving the other way. The trouble had caught others crossing the street and they were moving on now. Any one of the men might have cried Lou Hagerman's name at Lacy.

But the buggy held two women, and it was the pale oval of the slim girl's face that watched the walk edge where Hagerman moved. She looked as if something savage and strange stalked there. Hagerman touched his hat brim and she looked straight ahead. The older woman shook the reins and the buggy horse broke into a heavy trot.

Hagerman again had the disturbed feeling she knew why he was in Bitter Wells, and was therefore dangerous. But there was nothing he could do about it now. There was nothing he could do.

The Antler Hotel was on the corner where Jim Stel's Cinch Bar had stood years ago. New, wooden, two stories high, its verandah fronted on Main Street and ran around on the side street.

News could leap fast through a town. Men on the verandah and in the lobby knew this was Lon Hagerman, fresh from another gun play. Talk fell away when he walked in and asked for a room. Eyes were on his back as the clerk gave him a key and pointed to the red-carpeted stairs at the left of the small lobby.

Hagerman palmed the key and thoughtfully inquired: "Who's the sheriff?"

The clerk wore a stiff collar and purple sleeve bands and his small sandy mustache was carefully tended. He had a vain and sporty look. He wanted to be friendly with Lon Hagerman. His smirk was confidential,

"Will McCone's sheriff," he said, keeping it low, just for the two of them. "McCone won't worry you, Mister Hagerman. He's sick. Don't go out."

Hagerman said—"Thanks."—noncommittally, and left the

clerk smirking uncertainly across the register.

Hagerman locked the room door on the inside and tossed the suitcase, bouncingly on the brass bed. The room would do. It was another room in another town. He scarcely glanced at the furnishings as he hung his coat on the round brass knob of the footboard post and took a second shoulder rig and gun from the suitcase. And a box of cartridges.

Standing by the bed, he replaced the shell he'd fired at the young VP bully. On second thought he replaced the dead safety shell in each gun. Only then did he strip to the waist, carry razor and brush to the bright-oak washstand and framed mirror above it, and attack the train grime and stubble beginning to roughen his lean face.

He grinned faintly at the result in the mirror as he dried his face, then built a cigarette and sat on the bed edge, regretting the trouble with Lacy and his bunch. But it was done now, and it probably meant more trouble that he hadn't counted on. Hagerman shook his head.

Knuckles rapped on the door. He caught one of the guns off the bed and came silently to his feet, saying: "Yes?"

The hotel clerk's voice sounded as if he were speaking in a guarded simper, his mouth close to the door. "Message for you from a young lady."

Hagerman unlocked the door and stepped to one side. "Come in."

The clerk's knowing smile wiped off when the tall figure stripped to the waist demanded: "What young lady?"

The clerk swallowed. "She sent a boy to ask if you'd step out to the side hitch rack. She's in a buggy."

"No name?"

"Uh, no . . . just told the kid to say that. He's waiting downstairs."

"Tell him I'm coming." Hagerman's regard was reflective.

"Anything funny about it?"

"No, sir. Oh, no!"

"I didn't think so," Hagerman agreed, and judged the depart-
ing clerk would not think so again, either.

Both shoulder holsters were in place when Hagerman pulled
on his coat. He took a last look at himself in the mirror, a last
lick with the comb.

One, only one young lady would be waiting in a buggy for
Lon Hagerman. Anticipation stirred in Hagerman as he went
down the carpeted stairs.

Once more talk eased off as his impersonal gaze ran over the
faces in the lobby, on verandah, walk, and street. This was his
way always, but he watched now for the man he'd seen on the
station platform.

The lady's buggy was at the hitch rack on the side street, at
the far end, in shadows. And when Hagerman, hat in hand,
stepped out beside it, her request came coolly. "Will you come
with me to see Sheriff McCone?"

The buggy horse was old and leisurely as it turned along the
shadowy side street, avoiding the filled walks of Main Street.

"Most sheriffs would send a deputy," Hagerman remarked.
He was watching the shadows and occasional movements in the
night.

She said evenly: "I offered to come."

"His wife met the train?"

"Yes."

"Your mother?"

"I'm visiting the McCones."

Hagerman said gravely: "I'm Lon Hagerman, ma'am."

She caught his lurking amusement. "I'm Susan Kerr. And
I've heard of you, Mister Hagerman." It was the way she said it,
and the way she added: "You're quite. . . ."

Hagerman supplied it for her cheerfully: "Notorious?"

"Quite a killer," Susan Kerr finished stiffly.

"Not like you make it sound. I've been a peace officer twelve years, one way or another. Since I was eighteen. There's always trouble where I've served."

"Always trouble where you are. Always someone being killed." Dislike weighed her words. "Even when you come back to your own town." She drew a breath. "I warned Sheriff McCone of what I saw on the train. Missus McCone saw you start trouble with that rancher. You'd never seen him before, had you?"

"No," Hagerman admitted, and let it stand that way. Then he saw where they were and said: "Back of that big cottonwood is the old Stayer house. Kep Stayer and five of his outlaw bunch were caught hiding there. Old Sheriff Cotton Crockett deputized everyone in sight and surrounded the place at daybreak. A wind blew up. They couldn't fire the house without burning half the town. Couldn't get close enough all day to try it anyway. There were eleven dead by eight that night when the last of the Stayer bunch yelled quits out an upstairs window."

"You sound as if you enjoyed it," Susan Kerr said coldly.

"I remember it well enough. Before the Stayer man died, he admitted they'd meant to clean out the bank. They'd have left the town broke. Kep Stayer was a fox. His bunch killed quick and moved on fast."

Susan Kerr said intensely: "Women and children who lost husbands and fathers that day would rather the bank had been robbed."

"Families of men the Stayer bunch had killed other times might not," said Hagerman shortly. "Or families of men the gang would have killed later on. There's a price for everything. For peace. For safety. Bitter Wells stepped up and paid its price that day."

Beyond the next corner Susan Kerr drove into the yard of a neat white-painted clapboard house. They were walking to the steps when Susan stopped abruptly.

"A man like you can't understand," she said huskily. "My father was a sheriff. A decent kindly man. He had a killer deputy who started a gunfight one night, trying to make an arrest. When it was over, my father was dead. The deputy wasn't hurt. The killer had escaped."

Hagerman's sober look weighed her. "My father was one of the posse that the Stayer bunch killed. It decided me never to back away from an outlaw. To shoot first if one pulled a gun." Hagerman had never said this before. He closed it gruffly: "I'm satisfied."

They went silently onto the house porch. Silently Susan let him into the soft oil light of a pleasant little living room.

McCone, the Bitter Wells sheriff, was bedridden. A long, thin, spare man under the bed sheet. White fringed his uncut tow-colored hair. His eyes were blue, past the shaded bedside lamp, studying the visitor standing beside the bed.

"So you're Lon Hagerman?" The voice was clear, too, not like a sick man's voice. McCone was lean by nature, not illness, Hagerman guessed. McCone's hand clasp had strength. He lay propped well up on pillows, alertly weighing his visitor.

Mrs. McCone, without her yellow-feathered bonnet, had come out of the bedroom and with bare civility had ushered Hagerman in, and closed the door behind him. The two men were alone in the light cast by the bedside lamp.

"You left Bitter Wells before my time here," McCone said. "Made quite a name for yourself, for a fellow so young." The sheet, drawn over his chest, moved to shallow breathing as he paused. "Shoulder guns all the time?" he asked with professional interest.

"Mostly."

"You stepped off the train and shot a man."

"He bumped me and pulled his gun."

"Are you in Bitter Wells on business, Hagerman?"

"Call it looking around."

"My guess it's gun business."

Hagerman said easily: "Miss Kerr has her ideas. There were witnesses."

"You're clear on it," McCone admitted. He reached for tobacco sack and papers beside the lamp and smiled wryly. "Doc says not to smoke. So I do. Even a fool can be wise in his mistakes. It's all in why he makes them."

Hagerman smiled, too, wondering about McCone's purpose. McCone looked like a well man, kept his bed like an ill man, talked like a thoughtful man. He had, Hagerman guessed, little interest in Lacy's bullet-smashed hand.

McCone shaped a fat cigarette carefully, as if finding pleasure in rolling the forbidden smoke. He took two deep drafts, slowly, luxuriously, not looking up.

"I've heard all about the fight at the Stayer house," he said abruptly. "After your father was killed, you came to the fight with his rifle. Just a kid. They had to keep you from running at the house. Ever think what happened that day?"

"What's your idea?" Hagerman countered.

McCone said: "The Hagermans bought into this town with blood that day. It's the kind of buy that lasts."

"So?" asked Hagerman curiously.

"Bitter Wells has kept track of you. The great Lon Hagerman." McCone said it, smiling faintly.

Hagerman had the restless feeling the man was tolling him on for a purpose. He had his answer when McCone reached out beside the lamp, picked up a deputy's badge, and tossed it out on the sheet.

"Put it on," McCone said. He watched the instant shake of Hagerman's head, refusing. Emotion ran in McCone for the first time, sharpening his words. "Your town, Hagerman."

26

"No," denied Hagerman flatly. "I'm marshal at Silver Fork. Never came back, once I left."

The sharpness ran stronger in McCone.

"Your father stayed here for you. Dead. He bought into the town for you. What he did, stayed here for you. Now it's your turn."

Hagerman's hand brushed the words away. His statement was barely civil. "I don't know why you're in bed here, McCone. But if you can't hold your office, let them get a man who can."

The smile on McCone's face had its first bitterness. "I look good, don't I? The town thinks I've got stomach trouble." He tapped his chest. "Not even my wife knows. Only the doctor knows. The first exertion or excitement may finish me. Heart."

Hagerman's gesture regretted it. "Better quit. Or get good deputies."

"Here I am," said McCone. "Helpless and hiding it, so the wrong man won't get my job. I'm a dead man hanging on because it's best for the town. And I can't even tell the town about it. They think I'll be up again. My deputies can't handle the job. Or won't. Now you're here. Exactly what I need." McCone swallowed hard. "Like an answer to prayer."

"I've been called everything but an answer to prayer," Hagerman said. "Sorry, mister. Your business isn't my business."

McCone said steadily: "The big fellow you were watching through the train window is why I'm hanging onto my job. Vic Pauley."

"Pauley . . . so that's his name?" Hagerman said with soft satisfaction.

McCone was puzzled now. "You didn't know his name?"

"Only his face. And I never thought I'd find him in Bitter Wells." Hagerman took the badge off the bed sheet. "So you baited me on, knowing you'd hook me."

McCone said sharply: "No private grudges with that badge,

Hagerman."

They stared at each other. Hagerman jiggled the badge slowly in his palm. McCone watched the indecision hopefully. "Where is Pauley wanted?"

Hagerman let out a breath of regret. "Nowhere. There's nothing against him that would support a warrant. Just a friend of mine who sold his ranch and dropped by Silver Fork on his way to Denver to tell me about it, and was killed."

"Did Pauley kill him?"

"No proof. My friend had the money from his ranch sale. Paper money, mostly, in a money belt. He meant to marry a girl near Denver and buy the spread next to her father's ranch. He laughed when I warned him about carrying too much money in his belt. He was in love. He was happy."

"Lucky devil," said McCone.

"While it lasted," agreed Hagerman. "I had to ride out of town for a few hours. Coming back on the Bear Camp road that night, I met a rider and asked for a match. Next morning my friend was found in an alley, bashed on the head, finished with a knife, and his money belt gone. A barkeep remembered him having a drink with a stranger like the big fellow riding to Bear Camp. I never found that stranger, but I never forgot his face by match light. Tonight he walked outside the train window."

"Who was your friend, Hagerman?"

"Boy I went to school with. Tom Ashford. He inherited the Windowsash spread over on Rainbow Creek, and sold it." Hagerman tossed the badge back on the bed. "No proof in all that for a judge or jury. Any witnesses are long scattered. But Tom was my best friend when we were boys. Call it a private grudge."

McCone said from the pillows: "The VP ranch used to be the Windowsash. Vic Pauley bought it from Tom Ashford."

"So?" said Hagerman. "Pauley knew Tom's plans, I guess, and trailed him and got the ranch price back. A sharp business-man."

"Very sharp," McCone agreed. "After the ranch, Pauley bought an interest in two of the local saloons. When Metcalf, who owned the paper, died, Pauley bought it from the widow and brought in a man to run it. His money backs the gambling in two of the other saloons. Last spring he bought the Antler Hotel. I haven't proved anything . . . but rustling gets worse. There have been stage hold-ups. More hardcases seem to drift into town. I've been sick five months. They tell me things are getting out of hand. Pauley's newspaper has been suggesting my chief deputy, Red Gillis, would make a good sheriff."

"Sounds like Pauley is ready to take over," said Hagerman. He picked up the badge again. "Swear me in as your first deputy. Send word to the businessmen you can trust that I'm acting for you."

McCone's voice had a husky edge. "I've been stretched here, hanging on, waiting for a miracle."

"You'll have to wait for your miracle," Hagerman said bluntly. "I'm only Tom Ashford's friend." He rubbed his jaw slowly, squinting humorously down at McCone. "You could be a little right about buying into the town during the fight at the Stayer house."

McCone nodded, but his thoughts were elsewhere. "Be careful, Hagerman. Pauley will be wondering if you connect him with Ashford's murder."

Hagerman nodded. "I'm counting on it. He's guilty. It will eat at him. I'm betting it crowds him into a wrong move fast."

McCone agreed. "Any time now, Hagerman. Any hour. And it won't be in the open. He can't take a chance with you." McCone added wistfully: "And I can't get out and take a hand in it."

Hagerman chuckled. "You may be lucky, mister."

III

The next morning Hagerman was whistling softly under his breath when he entered the sheriff's office in the small brick courthouse.

Jiminy Jones, more like a mummy than ever, was lolling back before the roll-top desk, tobacco bulging one cheek. Jiminy hadn't worked since his pension started. He was the town loafer, knowing everything that happened.

"You're late," Jiminy reproved. "Red Gillis, who's been head deputy, done quit in a mad. He was seen ridin' toward Pauley's ranch."

Hagerman started a cigarette and grinned. "Jiminy, I need you on the payroll for extra eyes."

"I ain't workin' fer no one," declined Jiminy flatly. "But I can be handy. You tangled with a rough bunch last night. Looks like Red Gillis has throwed in with 'em. He's mean and fast with a gun, too. Here's your chair."

"Keep it. I won't be sitting much," Hagerman said. He flipped a match to the sand box. "Where's Vic Pauley?"

"Rode to the ranch late last night with his men."

Hagerman nodded, looked around the office, and sat in one of the straight chairs that creaked as he leaned back against the wall.

"I don't want any trouble with the VP men," he said mildly. "Got something else on my mind."

"Important?" Jiminy asked alertly.

"I'm looking for the man who murdered young Tom Ashford in Silver Fork several years ago."

"Holy cow. Here in Bitter Wells?"

"Around here."

"Don't want it told, I reckon?" Jiminy suggested reluctantly.

"Doesn't matter. I'm pretty sure who he is."

Hagerman smiled a little when old Jiminy quickly departed. Bitter Wells and the range would know fast that Lon Hagerman was trailing the killer of young Tom Ashford.

Hagerman sat considering the things McCone had told him. There was a part-time deputy, Sam Kinkaid, who ran a feed barn.

"Sam politicks. Gets votes. Folks like him," McCone had said. "But I wouldn't send him after a killer. Size Sam up yourself. He'll have a horse for you."

Hagerman stepped over to the gun rack on the wall and examined the rifles, carbines, and shotguns with the close interest of a man who lived or died by the weapons he carried.

Later, walking around town, he met people he remembered, who said they were glad to see him back, working with Will McCone.

But mostly talk died down and the covert impact of eyes was more watchful than friendly. Some of it was hostile. Long used to it, Hagerman was indifferent.

He was asked about Tom Ashford and shrugged, smiling. Jiminy Jones had gossiped fast.

Hagerman stopped at the feed barn. Sam Kinkaid was a medium-fleshed, hearty man, partly bald. His flow of talk reminded Hagerman of water splashing endlessly.

"I hear you're looking for a killer," said Kinkaid as they inspected horses in the pungent barn.

"Could be," said Hagerman blandly. "You might have a shotgun and some buckshot loads handy if those VP men come back to even up for last night."

Kinkaid swallowed. "They won't be back for trouble with Lon Hagerman."

Hagerman selected a big blue roan, a saddle with *tapaderos*, and walked out, satisfied. He had a good horse and had lost a deputy. Kinkaid was mostly talk.

In the afternoon he came opposite the Antler Hotel, where a six-horse stage was loading. Hagerman looked, and hastily crossed the street. Susan Kerr was in the vehicle. Hat in hand beside the wheel, Hagerman said: "I didn't know you were leaving."

Susan was cool. "I came to visit Nora McCone, who lives at Fort Frío." Her glance dropped to the bright deputy's badge. "You seem to be persuasive, Mister Hagerman. Nora will worry now. Her father will be held responsible for what you do."

Hagerman stood thinking of McCone's bad heart and stubborn holding of the sheriff's job, none of it known to his family.

"Tell Nora McCone not to worry," he said mildly. "Her father won't be hurt by what I do."

Susan didn't believe him.

Hagerman watched the lank and taciturn driver yell at his horses and swing the long whip, exploding over their ears, and the stage rolled fast out of town.

Bitter Wells, somehow, was different when he turned down the street. He had lost interest in the days ahead.

He was in the Boston Café just before dark, eating alone at a rear table, thinking about Susan Kerr, when old Jiminy Jones plunged in the front door and looked wildly around. Hagerman stood up.

Jiminy called the length of the room excitedly: "Lon! The driver an' a passenger was killed on the Frío stage! The other passengers just got the stage back to the hotel!"

Hagerman ran to the front, the café in turmoil around him. "What passenger was killed?" he demanded harshly. And again: "Who was it?"

"Feller named Clinch, runs sheep t'other side of the Frío!" Jiminy panted.

Hagerman bolted out. Others were running on the walk

ahead of him. The stage was where it had loaded, only four horses in the harness now. Two bodies lay slackly on top of the coach. The five remaining passengers were hemmed in by the growing crowd. Hagerman shoved through to them.

Susan's pale, blazing indignation greeted him. "They were murdered by two drunken thieves. They didn't have a chance."

Hagerman got the story in quick, indignant fragments from all the passengers. Buckshot blasts had killed driver, a horse, and the sheepman riding beside the driver before the stage had had a chance to stop.

Two men had done it. Two men, bandanna-masked, jeering, threatening as they lined passengers beside the stage and took valuables. The taller of the two had called a threat as he backed off with his shorter companion: "Tell the sheriff if he crawls outta bed after us, we'll shoot his ears into hoss-thief jingle-bobs."

Susan said with tight-lipped intensity: "They were drunken cowhands. Brutes."

A lean, shocked-looking drummer said: "They were too drunk to hold their tongues. The tall one staggered, and the other one swore at him and said . . . 'Sober up, you fool, or you won't make it past the high water tonight.' "

"The high water?" Hagerman repeated sharply.

Jiminy Jones jogged his elbow. "Lon. There ain't ary high water they could ride to tonight but the falls up Turkey Creek. Usta be a little bob-tailed, hard-rock mine back up in there. Ain't hardly a trail to it now. But there's shelter up there where two gunnies could hide out."

"They're drunk and a posse could catch them," Susan blazed.

A lanky young man with red stubble on a long flat face spoke sarcastically from the crowd: "Since when did Hagerman need a posse to bring in two drunks?"

Hagerman cocked a glance at the speaker and stood in the

deep dusk, thinking. His smile came slow and thin. "That's right. Two drunks don't call for a posse." He sensed relief in the men standing near.

"Drunk or sober, they're killers," Susan reminded.

"Makes us even then," Hagerman told her. "Don't worry, ma'am, I won't shoot first."

"You'd better shoot first," Susan warned. She was pale and still upset. She had seen death, cold-blooded and needless.

Hagerman turned away, smiling a little, and shouldered through the crowd, and found Jiminy Jones still at his heels.

"Lon, you damn' fool. That strawberry rooster who egged you on is Ham Gillis, cousin to Red Gillis. He ain't a friend. Up to'ard that old mine is worse'n a trap, with two likkered thieves watchin' their back trail. Hell of a note. I still got to keep an eye on you."

Hagerman grinned. "Jiminy, I'd like to know what Cousin Gillis does next."

"You'll know," Jiminy promised, and turned hastily back.

Only a hostler was at Kinkaid's feed barn. The courthouse was dark, save for lamplight in the sheriff's office as Hagerman went to the gun rack.

He had a cartridge belt strapped under his coat, Winchester in the saddle scabbard, sawed-off double-barreled shotgun tied behind the saddle, as the big blue roan turned into Main Street, worrying the restraining bit, wanting to run.

Half the town seemed to be on the walks, watching him pass. They were quiet. They did not call out encouragement. They were no part of the rider or his errand. Hagerman had ridden out in this solitary way many times in the past. It went with being Lon Hagerman. He could have wished it different tonight. Wished for warmth, friendship as they watched him go. This had been his town.

Jiminy Jones's thin, stooped figure darted out into the street and Hagerman pulled up. Jiminy spoke under his breath at the right stirrup. "He lit a shuck outta town."

"Thanks, Jiminy."

Hagerman rode on, not bothering to look at the walks now. His face had settled into hard, watchful lines. He was a solitary, stern, rather lonely figure as the roan struck a long lope out of town, into the night shrouding the Fort Frío road.

When the town lights were pinpoint winks dropping behind low brushy ridges, Hagerman reined off to the right, on a narrow, rough wagon trail.

This had been his country. He hardly needed the dim starlight to keep the roan in a high run. In an hour he was at the Rainbow Creek ford of the Frío cut-off trail which he had been following. He let the blowing horse drink sparingly, and stood quietly at the creek edge, listening.

Finally he risked matches, cupped in palms above the trail marks at the water's edge. Satisfied, he rode through the gurgling current and bore left over a sage flat to higher grassy coulées. He passed cattle. Twice he opened wire gates that had been in these back-ranch fences when he was a boy.

Riding slower, he topped a brushy ridge and pulled up, studying faint window glow on a flat below. He walked the horse slowly down dim corrals. One corral held four horses. The others were empty.

Hagerman tied the roan to a pole of an empty corral, unlashed the sawed-off shotgun, and slipped in two buckshot shells as he walked quietly to the front of the house.

It was adobe, little changed. Hagerman knew each room inside. He made sure there was no horse tied out front. The roan nickered loudly back at the corral.

A man's shadow moved across one of the shade-covered windows. Hagerman stepped to the front door and knocked, and leaned the shotgun beside the door, and stood with his coat front slackly open.

Steps came. The door swung open. Hagerman requested mildly: "Got a match, mister, before you ride on to Bear Camp?"

The big-chested muscular man stood motionlessly, peering, his face in shadow. He wore a gun, but made no move toward it.

"You're Hagerman, who shot my foreman last night," he finally said slowly.

"You're Pauley, who knifed Tom Ashford at Silver Fork," Hagerman said in the same mild tone. "I'm deputy for Will McCone now, and Tom Ashford was my old friend. Step out and we'll start riding."

Vic Pauley's stunned moment passed. "That's a fool charge!" he exclaimed.

"I'm in a hurry, come along," Hagerman ordered. "Take your choice about trying for your gun or making a break while we ride. I'll be close with double-barreled buckshot."

Pauley's hard laugh settled that. "A gun? Hell, my lawyer in Bitter Wells is all I need. Let's go." Then, outside the doorway, Pauley halted abruptly. "You want me out on the road, to shoot me in the back, and claim I tried an escape?"

"Be a pleasure," said Hagerman briefly. "I've thought about Tom Ashford a long time. But I don't wear a law badge that way."

Reassured, Pauley stalked back to the corrals.

"I'll take your gun now," Hagerman said. He got it, and stood watchfully with the saw-off shotgun while Pauley caught a horse and saddled and swung up.

"Ride the back pasture trail to Bear Cañon Mesa," Hagerman ordered.

"That's away from Bitter Wells," Pauley protested in new alarm.

"Ride, mister," Hagerman said with his first cold impatience.

"I've other business before I get you locked up in town. You're safe unless you make a break."

Pauley said with stifled rage: "All I want is my lawyer and the judge to hear him."

IV

They rode smartly, Pauley leading, and conscious of the buckshot close behind him by the way he kept looking back.

They had a pale moon as the horses crossed Bear Mesa at a long lope. When they pulled up for a breather, Hagerman directed: "Cut around Bald Ridge and find the old wood wagon trail going out to the Fort Frío road."

"You going to Fort Frío?" Pauley demanded sullenly.

"Just ride, mister!"

Wood wagons had kept the old trail open. The horses dropped fast down a last rough grade to moonlight glinting on a shallow, fast-running stream ford and stopped to snatch water. It was near midnight.

"Turn upstream," Hagerman directed.

Vic Pauley's hulk twisted sharply in the saddle. "That goes up into Turkey Cañon."

"Get going."

"Nothing up there."

"Who said there was? Get going."

Pauley sat stiffly on his horse, protesting with his first real emotion. "Hagerman, you mean to kill me."

"I could have shot you any time in the last two hours if I was minded. Get moving!"

Vic Pauley reined his horse upstream in a kind of numb helplessness, as if confused. A trail of sorts kept close to the brawling water. Wooded slopes began to draw in. The mountains piled high and black before them.

They began to pass pines and skirted a first sheer rise of

rock. Pauley suddenly pulled his horse to a stop. His thick voice protested: "Do this later, Hagerman. Your business isn't mine. Get me into your damned jail. I'm sick."

Hagerman was mildly sympathetic. "Fresh air should help you. After we look around up here, you can stop in town and see the doctor."

"I can't make it," Pauley insisted hoarsely.

Hagerman thought it over and cocked the sawed-off shotgun. The sharp click struck into Pauley's rigid waiting.

"We'll ride on," Hagerman decided. "Make a sound, Pauley, any sound, until I order it, and I'll blow your backbone through your belly. Try me if you think I won't. Ride slow, just in front of me."

A man could groan silently with every set of his head and shoulders and slow unwilling movements. Pauley did so as he rode on with a stiff, unnatural, shrinking look, his head turned a little, as if listening to the night ahead. He rode in fear, and looked it.

Hagerman watched the blurred figure, limned occasionally as moonlight struck into the deepening cañon. He wished Tom Ashford could see this. His thoughts jumped back to Bitter Wells, and the loneliness of being Lon Hagerman came at him hard now.

They were following the roughest kind of trail up into the cañon. Hagerman finally caught a far whisper murmuring toward them. That would be Turkey Creek Falls. The high water.

He'd been watching the roan's ears testing the night. He reached suddenly to loosen the saddle carbine in the scabbard, and crowded the roan up close behind Pauley's horse.

Thin brush grew along here and scrawny pines lifted from among great tumbled boulders. To the left the growing creek had cut its deep channel. To the right the slope angled up, then rose steeply with its cover of rooted pines.

There was no bright moonlight here in the cañon bottom. Pauley was a dim, hulking blot, sitting stiffly in the saddle as he rode through raking brush into open space beyond.

It was from there the rough demand came from the boulder-clogged slope to the right: "Lon Hagerman?"

Hagerman was unloading in a cat-like swing on the opposite side of the roan as he called: "It's Hagerman! Come out!"

Vic Pauley's frantic yell rang over it. "Don't shoot, boys! This is . . . !"

Rifle shots crashed over Pauley's voice. Shots from half a dozen spots on the steep boulder-strewn slope to the right.

Hagerman landed hard and stumbled over a dead branch. Pauley's protest chopped off while the guns still crashed. The roan horse lunged and reared, snorting wildly. It had been hit. Hagerman's shotgun roared twice, and he faded fast into the deep shadows of the brush from which they had just issued.

"Tex got a face full of buckshot! He's gone!"

Another voice called from the slope ahead. "Sounded like Vic Pauley!"

Flat on the ground in the brush, Hagerman reloaded the shotgun. The roan had fallen. Pauley's horse had bolted on up the cañon.

Hagerman had no emotion now. He'd guessed it would be like this. There were more guns than he'd expected. They hadn't taken chances.

They had him—*or* Lon Hagerman had them. What had McCone said? Even a fool could be wise in his mistakes, depending on why he made them.

"They ain't no one moving!"

"Go look, Lacy! You meant to shoot Hagerman first with your good left hand!"

"Pauley put Red Gillis in charge! Gillis, drag Hagerman's meat out in the open! We'll keep you covered!"

A gasping cough came off the ground near the fallen roan horse. "You fools shot me! I'm Pauley! Get Hagerman!"

"Pauley! What'n hell's he doin' up here with Hagerman?"

Hagerman was crawling upslope. He had the Colt guns inside his coat, the buckshot gun in his hand. Their horses would be up the cañon. He had the way out blocked until they killed him.

A tiny dead stick cracked weakly under his knee. A rifle hammered lead at the sound. Other guns joined in. Bullets ripped through the brush, close. Then silence, waiting, listening.

"I heard somethin'!"

"Your belly quakin', Slim, over killin' them two on the stage! Wasn't no need for that! Hagerman would 'a' come anyway!"

"Tell it to Tex! He did it."

"Tex looks dead now. Feels like it, too. He always was cold-blooded."

Hagerman inched up the slope, up above the brush.

"You reckon Hagerman's dead?"

"If he ain't, he lit out afoot."

Hagerman was roughly abreast of them on the slope. He located a fist-sized rock and stood cautiously. The rock landed noisily down the brush.

Guns clamored and crashed. Hagerman drove both barrels of buckshot along the slope, and lunged on up the slope, tossing the shotgun aside for the six-guns in his shoulder holsters.

He'd drawn a scream of pain, alarmed shouts, rifle lead tearing across the spot where the shotgun had spoken. Footsteps didn't matter now. The guns and shouts covered minor sounds.

The men were shifting position, scattering up the slope. Hagerman saw a muzzle blast close. He triggered both guns at it and ran in toward the spot. He stumbled over a body. Still moving, he went into a crouch and fired at another red muzzle spurt.

There had been five or six of them left, all wanting Lou

Hagerman. Now he was in among them. Every man was a target. But they weren't sure which guns were Lon Hagerman's.

Lead screamed off a big rock alongside him and ripped up his arm. Still moving, Hagerman fired at another muzzle flame and ducked on along the slope. His foot struck another body. Their guns were blasting at their own guns. He dropped flat again, catching his breath.

Well on ahead he heard a shout. "Pauley's dead! Who we fightin' for?"

The last shots died away. Stumbling feet were running upcañon. Voices were shouting back and forth. Hagerman reloaded the Colt guns and started back for the shotgun.

He was still trying to locate it when he heard the furious run of approaching horses. He cocked the six-guns and hunkered behind a rock upslope from the open space where the trap had waited. The first dark blot of horse and rider burst into view, rider bending low, spurring desperately past the slope of death.

Hagerman opened fire as three other pounding blurs followed close. Their guns blasted back at him. One man shouted and pitched off into the brush where Hagerman had hidden. The other three went on in a crashing rush down Turkey Creek Cañon, fear driving them. That was one reward of being Lon Hagerman. Break up a bunch like that and they'd have enough of Hagerman.

He sat behind the rock, reloading the guns again from force of habit. A groan lifted on along the slope. "I'll get to you!" Hagerman called. "Lay easy and keep away from a gun."

There would be horses still tied up the cañon. And a mess here to clean up. Maybe more than one wounded man to pack back. Hagerman leaned back against the big rock. He was suddenly tired.

He listened suddenly to the thin far echo of shots drifting up the cañon. More guns than the three fleeing riders had with them.

Silence fell as Hagerman stood up. He picked his way slowly down the rough slope and stood listening.

Then he heard a far shout and relaxed. It called: "Hagerman! Lon Hagerman!"

He fired two signal shots, heard an answer, and quickly heard riders coming fast. He was beside the trail, feeling his wounded arm, when they rode crackling through the brush and pulled up around him. Eight of them, Hagerman counted.

It was old Jiminy Jones who said: "Here's part o' your posse, Lon! Three come hellin' at us, shootin' when they seen us. We got 'em. Any more around?"

"No more to worry about," said Hagerman. "Vic Pauley had a trap set here. Pauley was the one who killed Tom Ashford. He couldn't wait to see what I'd do about it. The stage hold-up was bait to pull me in. A deputy shot down while trailing two drunken killers would have settled everything for Pauley."

Hagerman was speaking without emotion. "So I cut over to Pauley's ranch to see how he felt about it. At the Frío cut-off ford on Rainbow Creek, there was wet trail sign where a bunch of riders had crossed the creek, heading toward the Fort Frío road or Turkey Creek. Men never much rode that way at night. I found Pauley alone at his ranch and brought him along to see what was up the cañon here."

"He want to come?" one of the men asked.

"He came," said Hagerman briefly. "He couldn't say why he shouldn't come, without talking about the hold-up and the trap he'd baited for me. So we rode up here," Hagerman said without regret, "and his men killed him by mistake." Hagerman looked up at the riders bulking darkly around him.

"I didn't expect to have a posse following," he remarked.

"That girl, that Miss Kerr, talked it up," said Jiminy Jones.

"She went to Will McCone, an' he sent fer friends. McCone kinda guessed like you did. He said the hold-up an' all smelled like trouble to him. But the gal shamed 'em all, by jiminy. I heered her. She said it was a poor town that'd let a deputy ride out alone at night after two killers. Told 'em they didn't deserve Lon Hagerman."

The man next to Jiminy laughed sheepishly. "She had a tongue and a temper. So we come on to help."

"Well now, that's fine," Hagerman said. He chuckled. "Miss Kerr must have been persuasive."

Jiminy said: "You oughta heard her. Oughta thank her for it."

They couldn't see Hagerman's growing smile in the dark. But it was in his voice. A new warmth, he could feel strongly. "That's fine," Hagerman said again. "Fine. We've got a little clean-up to do here, and then we'll get on home."

He liked the sound of that. Home.

"Soon as we get home, friends," Hagerman promised, "I'll see the young lady."

★ ★ ★ ★ ★

Death Takes a Tally

★ ★ ★ ★ ★

Ted Flynn completed this story on February 20, 1940. His agent, Marguerite E. Harper, had an agreement with Jack Burr, editor of Street & Smith's *Western Story,* to submit regularly stories by her three principal writers of Western fiction, Peter Dawson, Luke Short, and T. T. Flynn, and so Flynn knew beforehand where this story would be going. He also knew what Jack Burr wanted most: action and realistic violence. After commission, he received $341.16 for "Death Takes a Tally," which appeared in the issue dated July 27, 1940 where T. T. Flynn's name was in first position of the three included on the cover illustrated by a picture of a cowboy surveying a huge body count. Inside, Flynn's story, billed as a "book-length novel," appeared at the top of the Table of Contents.

I

Mike McBride was twenty-one this second day of the beef drive when the black clouds hung low from Big Baldy to the Screwjack Hills far south. And now and then the clouds dropped marching veils of mist and fine rain into which the big Circle 8 steers plodded with lowered heads.

Twenty-one this day—and under a down-pulled black hat and gay, closely woven blanket poncho, Mike McBride was singing as he spurred the chunky claybank ahead toward Larrupin' Ed Shaw, who was riding point.

You could feel like singing on a day like this. You didn't care whether it was sleeting or snowing, raining or sunny when you'd become twenty-one and half of a beef drive was your birthday present. Half of six hundred and twenty-eight head by the final tally as they strung off the home ground for the leisurely two weeks' drive to the Two Rivers shipping pens. Prime steers for the most part, with a few old mossy bulls and cows that had been hazed out of the Salt Creek brakes.

Concho Walker had promised it three days ago, before riding to Salt Fork with the wagon and old Jump-John Myers.

"You're plenty man already, Mike, but it'll be legal-like afore Jump-John an' I meet the drive at Dripping Springs with the wagon." Concho's gnarled hand had reached for tobacco and brown papers as he growled: "Don't seem no time since you was that tough, hungry little button that the blizzard blowed in to help me 'n' Jump-John save them cattle."

47

Mike had grinned reminiscently as he stood, wiry and lean, gray eyes level with old Concho's faded stare.

"Seems to me like it was a long time ago," Mike had said. "A heap has happened since."

Concho had twisted the end of his smoke deliberately and lighted it before he spoke. "Uhn-huh. A heap. You was just shadin' twelve. 1 wa'n't but a busted-down old brush squatter with a measly beef bunch that wa'n't even paid for. Salt Fork was half a dozen shacks, an' free grass laid from the Baldy range to the Screwjack *malpais.*"

"I must've brought the rush." Mike had chuckled. "Look at Salt Fork now . . . six saloons, a bank, a sheriff, an' a boothill. Every time I ride out, I hear someone else has come into the country."

Concho's seamed old face had darkened at things he hated.

"Gittin' so a ranny cain't roll out o' his soogans an' stretch without pokin' some stranger in the eye. Good thing I got here first an' took my pick." Then Concho had shrugged. "We've done all right, I reckon. The Circle Eight has got grass an' water, an' the beef drive this year'll bring us good cash money to bank. We've worked hard an' et old jerky an' bad beans long enough. The hard days is done. We're in the tall grass an' clover. An' you've more'n done your share, Mike. All them lean years without wages, same as Jump-John an' me. So I'm gonna start you out a man with half the steer money in the Two Rivers Bank to your name."

Mike had flared back quickly: "Who wants any cash money in the bank? You think I've been hanging around for a big hunk of the fat meat?"

"Shut up!" Concho had snapped. "I know what I'm a-doin'! An like I told you-all this mornin', I'm leavin' you men to get the drive under way while I ride to Salt Fork with Jump-John an' the wagon. We'll meet you at the springs."

"The way you cussed Salt Fork last time you come back," Mike had observed, "I wouldn't figure you'd hone to see it before Two Rivers."

"Don't care if I never see it again," Concho had growled. "Just lookin' at the place gets me feelin' crowdy. But I got business to do, an' I might as well get it over with. Maybe you an' me'll ride on from Two Rivers after the steers is sold. It's time a younger feller like you shoved cash money in his pocket an' looked around. You been workin' too hard on the Circle Eight fer years now."

"I've been getting out. Last year I rode to El Paso an' Santa Fe."

"I ain't askin' where you been," Concho had snapped. "I'm tellin' you what you'll probably do. You ain't big enough yet to stand an' argy with me. I told you . . . an' that's how it'll be. Dern that lead in my shoulder. It's gonna rain."

Well, that was old Concho, snorting and a-bellowing like a tailed-up bull for fear someone would find how soft he was inside. But Mike McBride knew. Even now, as he spurred his claybank through a spit of rain, Mike's throat tightened at the thought of that birthday present.

Many a man worked hard all his life and never laid hands on so much money. It was wealth for a young buster just twenty-one. And hard to believe even now. Mike hadn't expected it.

Years back, when that hard-shelled button wearing too-big hand-me-downs had ridden out of the storm on a stolen horse, the Circle 8 sod cabin and the gaunt, stooped old brush buster had meant only warmth and grub for a few days until the weather faired. Helping hold the sorry bunch of cows from a disastrous drift had been no more than even trade for grub. But the "few days" had stretched into weeks, months, years. The button and the Circle 8 had grown together.

Old Concho Walker had been one of Quantrill's riders, and

before and after that a freighter, gambler, cowhand, handy with a gun from the Mexican settlements in California to the rip-roaring spot on Cherry Creek that had turned into the silver-and-cattle town called Denver. Concho had come out of it all an old man with empty pockets, and lead scattered in his tall gaunt frame to ache when the weather was bad.

But land and cattle of his own had done something to the old man. Winter evenings when Concho told yarns of the past he talked calmly, as a man might speak of things some other man had lived through. Yet when he talked of the Circle 8, Concho's faded, squinty eyes glowed and his voice grew eager.

"I had to live to be an old fool afore I dropped my loop on a good thing, button. A man ain't a man until his feet stand hard on his own land. The Circle Eight ain't much now, but she's a-gettin' bigger each year. Like you, button. Ain't no tellin' what a young 'un or a good cow spread'll grow into if they're handled right. Jest keep your eye peeled an' watch."

Staying around to watch the Circle 8 grow had seemed natural to Mike McBride. Before a fellow knew it the Circle 8 was home, the Circle 8's good luck and bad luck were part of life.

You sort of forgot that all men weren't square and generous like old Concho, that life was wolf-eat-wolf, that when you grew up you were going to outwolf them all because of those early years when you'd been kicked around by bigger wolves.

Times you did think about it you were confident you'd out-wolf them all when old Concho didn't need you any more and you finally left the Circle 8. You'd grown to handle guns in a way that made even Concho grunt with approval. Your half-starved kid body had grown fast to stocky, tireless manhood.

Concho didn't know about that saloon trouble in El Paso last fall that would have ended in gun trouble if Mike McBride's fists hadn't beaten a border tough helpless, and then the tough's partner, reeling and dazed, before either man could snatch his gun.

Concho and old Jump-John and the newer hands, Larrupin' Ed Shaw, Slim Chance, Gus Delight, Jim Crowder, and Sam Parks never suspected the cold, wolfish delight that flooded Mike McBride when he thought of that savage saloon fight that had left him cock of the walk and ready for more trouble—gun trouble if anyone asked for it.

The wolf pup had become a he-wolf ready for the pack. But now, as Mike stopped singing and stared into the misty rain, throat tight at the thought of those steers that were his birthday present, he felt less like a he-wolf than at any time he could remember.

Concho had given more than prime steers, more than money in the bank, or friendship and hearty words. A part of the old man had reached out to something in Mike McBride that had been frozen, aloof, coldly vengeful ever since, as a terrified kid just coming on eight, he had seen his mother butchered by renegades masquerading as raiding Kiowas.

As Mike rode up, Larrupin' Ed Shaw observed: "You shore pick purty weather to bust out singin' like a canary. Better save it for your night trick in case we git thunder an' lightning. Them old mossybacks is still mad an' boogery an' layin' off to lead a run."

"I've got plenty left over." Mike chuckled. "Ain't you heard this is a birthday?"

Larrupin' Ed hunched under his yellow slicker, wet hat brim drooping and water trickling off his long mustache as he grumbled: "When you git old as I am, you'll groan on your birthdays, kid. Concho knowed what he was about when he went around by Salt Fork with the wagon. Bet he's bellied up to a dry bar now, swappin' lies over a whiskey bottle."

"Concho ain't had a drink in years," Mike reminded.

Larrupin' Ed shifted in the saddle and snorted.

"Ain't because he didn't want it. Concho's been takin' his likker kick in buildin' up his cow spread. An' gettin' drier every year like a desert weed in a drought. When it comes time for rain, Concho's dry roots is gonna soak up everything in sight." Larrupin' Ed shook water off his mustache and chuckled grimly. "I've seen 'em dry out like that before. An' when they finally git set under a gentle pour o' whiskey, they sprout flowers an' green leaves an' howl. I hear Concho talkin' about the hard days bein' over. If that ain't medicine talk to break a drought, I never heered none. And I kin spot a sly look in that old coon's eye. He had somethin' on his mind when he lit out fer Salt Fork. It weren't grub fer us or dodgin' a wet saddle out here with the drive, either."

"It's your own tongue that's hanging dry." Mike grinned. "Salt Fork ain't the place Concho'll go to do his drinking. He ain't liked Salt Fork since it growed up fast so close under his nose. If he was in Two Rivers, now, with the steers sold, you might be guessing right. Concho's earned a case of likker the way he's worked an' done without."

"Why'd he have to go to Salt Fork, then?"

"Had business there. Maybe at the new courthouse."

"Have it your way." Larrupin' Ed shrugged. "We'll know when we meet the wagon at Drippin' Springs tomorrow night. . . . Say, didja hear *that?*"

Two faint gunshots had come soggily through the mist veils hiding the brushy country through which the drive had just come.

"Sounded like a signal," Mike said, twisting in the saddle and staring back.

Gus Delight and Sam Parks, riding swing, were looking back, also.

Several moments passed, and then two more shots rapped

unmistakably far back of where Slim Chance was bringing up the drag.

"Trouble!" Larrupin' Ed jerked out. "An' a little more of that shootin' close in'll send them mossyhorns hightailin'! Better git back an' see what's wrong!"

Mike was already reining hard back past the noisy, nervous cattle, past Gus Delight, who was riding fast to head off an old cow and trying to look back toward the gunshots at the same time. Back past the drags that had started to fan out from the gunfire behind them.

Slim Chance wasn't at his post, keeping them bunched and moving ahead. Slim might have been shot off his horse.

But the horse wasn't in sight, either, as two more shots cracked sharply. Mike galloped all of two hundred yards on the back trail before he made out Slim's riderless black pony beyond a chaparral clump.

Swearing, Mike had his belt gun out from under the blanket poncho before he saw Slim getting to his feet on the other side of the horse. Beyond the chaparral clump a second horse was easily recognizable as Concho's pet Gray Star. Then Mike saw that a man was visible, lying at Slim's feet.

II

Mike swore again as he raced close enough to note the stricken worry on Slim's angular face. Concho hurt out here, miles from Dripping Springs, where he was to have met the drive.

Mike brought the running horse up short and hit the muddy ground before he saw that the prone man was old Jump-John Myers.

"Plugged in the lungs an' hip," Slim said hoarsely. "Look at him."

It was there plain enough to see. Old Jump-John, white-haired, bowlegged, stooped. He was older than Concho and not good for much any more but droll humor and driving a wagon and helping cook. Old Jump-John, with his slicker muddy and blood-smeared, and the crimson froth of his life bubbling on a slack mouth as the misty rain patted unnoticed on his wide, staring eyes.

"He must've cut our sign back there a piece an' burred on his horse until he sighted the drag," Slim said huskily. "Guess he couldn't make it any more an' dragged his gun an' shot as he took a header off the hoss. He's been tryin' to tell me something about Concho, but he chokes up an' can't get it out."

Jump-John was choking again as Mike knelt in the mud. Rattling gasps shook the frail, hunched figure. Jump-John was strangling on his own weakness and blood, and not much could be done about it. There wasn't any way to get a doctor, and probably not even enough time to call back the grub wagon that was far ahead with the remuda, and give the dying man shelter.

Mike lifted the old man's head a little. It helped. Jump-John got his throat clear, drew a sobbing breath, and gathered his strength with visible effort. His harsh whisper was dear enough. "Git to Salt Fork an' stop Concho. He done a little business an' took a drink an' was off like a wild man. Celebratin' about his son, he was whoopin' fer the whole damn' town to drink to the feller who's a big cattleman."

Slim, bending over the spot, heard him and whistled. "Concho never mentioned no son. Always acted like he'd never been married."

"I told him so, an' he called me a ole fool an' yelled fer me to drink to the boy," Jump-John gasped. "Concho's throwed his loop on a hellacious drunk that's gotta be stopped."

"He have a gunfight before you left?" Mike demanded.

Jump-John rolled his head weakly in a negative. "I seen he

was set to stay in Salt Fork an' likely drink er gamble the Circle Eight away, so I got his hoss out o' the livery stable an' started to head you boys off an' git someone to stop him afore the tinhorn gamblers got at him. An' just this side of the Salt Fork crossin' by the Black Butte, I was bushwhacked. Feller plugged me twicet with a rifle an' then rode up to make sure I was a goner."

Jump-John choked and gasped again, and, when the spasm passed, he was vastly weaker. Mike had to bend low to hear now.

"Never seen the feller before. Look, near big pine. He should've . . . kept away."

"Why'd he shoot you?" Mike asked. "Can you hear me, John? Why'd he shoot you?"

Jump-John heard, for his head moved in another negative. But his gasping whisper was not the reply. "Git Concho afore it's too late. I'm afeered. . . ."

Jump-John choked again, and Mike's eyes were smarting and he was swearing in husky helplessness as he watched the old man go quiet and inert in the circle of his arm.

Larrupin' Ed came riding up as Mike lowered his burden to the wet, yellow slicker, and stood up.

"I heered more shots! What the devil is it?" Larrupin' Ed yelled as he rode up.

"Jump-John was bushwhacked. There's trouble in Salt Fork. Circle the cattle an' get the wagon back here for a burying." Mike threw harshly at the older man: "I'm riding to Salt Fork."

But Larrupin' Ed was already swinging down.

"Bushwhacked? Who bushwhacked him?"

"He didn't get it out."

Larrupin' Ed's long black mustache jerked as he looked down at Jump-John and began to swear bitterly.

"How come someone shot a harmless old feller like him?

Where's the wagon? Where's Concho? Ain't that his horse?"

"Concho's in Salt Fork on a drunk," Mike said hoarsely. "Something to do with a son he never told us about. Jump-John figgered he'd better get word to us an' started on Concho's horse. He was bushwhacked this side of the Salt Fork crossing. That's all we got from him. Jump-John never carried money enough to earn a killing, an' never made trouble."

"On Concho's hoss it might be he was mistook for Concho," Larrupin' Ed suggested.

"Concho was raising hell in Salt Fork," Mike reminded bitterly. "Why would anybody be at the Salt Fork crossing looking for him?"

"It must've been a mistake," Slim put in heavily. "Concho ner Jump-John never riled anyone enough to bring on a killin' this way."

"Mistake, hell!" Mike said violently. "You don't make a mistake down a rifle barrel in daytime. Not twice. You know damn' well who you're shooting an' why. Jump-John was killed because he was Jump-John. An' the reason's back there in Salt Fork, where Concho's blown his top over this son that's turned up. You men'll have to bury Jump-John. I'm going to Salt Fork for the answer."

Mike was swinging in the saddle as he finished. Larrupin' Ed plunged over to his stirrup.

"Wait'll we get the drive stopped an' the wagon back here an' I'll side you, Mike," he urged.

"Stay with the cattle," Mike told him. "Better push on to the springs for the water an' grass. I'll bring Concho to the springs. Might as well bury Jump-John here. He was like Concho. Always wanted to be off alone a heap. I'll get my rifle and turn the remuda back."

Before Larrupin' Ed could answer, Mike was spurring away. Gus Delight saw him coming and rode back to meet him.

Jump-John's death made Gus erupt in profane anger. A signal caught Sam Parks's attention. Larrupin' Ed galloped up. Mike tarried long enough to help start the big steers circling, and then went on to get his rifle, and turn back the wagon and remuda.

Jump-John had died late in the afternoon. Dark had just closed down, the rain had stopped, and patches of moonlight were gleaming through holes in the clouds when the Black Butte loomed off to Mike's right with cloud streamers drifting past the top like strands of misty hair.

Jump-John had said to look near a big pine. Many pines grew near Black Butte, and more than one big pine stood near the trail. The soggy ground was dark and there was little chance to find what Jump-John had been talking about.

Mike turned off the trail to several of the big pines without much hope of seeing anything. It was as good a way as any to spell his horse. And it was the horse, snorting, shying from something on the ground, that located the body Mike would have missed.

A flaring match showed the man lying face down on the wet pine needles, black hat half crushed under his head. Mike rolled him over. Another match made clear the thin, fox-like face with a loose mouth under a neat brown mustache.

A two-gun man. One gun was still in the hand-stamped leather holster, the other lay beside the body. A bullet had struck beside the left nostril and come out the back of the head.

This was what Jump-John had tried to tell about, what Jump-John had meant when he said the stranger should have kept away.

Mike stood there in the black night, picturing old Jump-John galloping hard from the Salt Fork crossing while this fox-faced gunman carefully sighted a rifle and fired the death bullet.

Old Jump-John must have tried to reach cover. The second shot, perhaps, had knocked him out of the saddle under the pine. Like a dead man, old Jump-John must have lain here while the stranger came up to make sure the job was done right. Then old Jump-John had nailed him squarely in the face.

Old-timers like Jump-John and Concho were rawhide tough. Jump-John had been tough enough to get back on his horse and ride on to find the Circle 8 drive.

The dead man, Mike discovered, wore a money belt that held several hundred dollars in gold and a deputy sheriff's badge. Mike was frowning as he put the badge back and shoved the money belt in one of the saddle pockets. If the dead man was a deputy, why wasn't he wearing his badge? If he wasn't a deputy, why was he carrying the badge in his money belt?

Answers to those questions were no clearer than old Jump-John's murder. The dead man's horse was gone. Wandered away, probably, carrying the rifle that had killed Jump-John.

Mike was turning back for a final look at the body when his claybank nickered loudly. And over to the left, back in the trees, another horse nickered.

At the first sound Mike snatched his belt gun and jumped for the trailing reins. Then he listened. It might be the dead man's horse, still tied where the owner had left him before ambushing Jump-John,

The horses nickered again and wind shook drops from the trees in ghostly pattering. Then silence fell again. The clouds parted and let silver moonlight drench the spot as Mike moved to mount and ride to the other horse.

A sharp, high voice behind the big pine froze his movement. "You're covered with a rifle! Stand still!"

III

Under his breath, Mike damned the bright moonlight that made him a clear target to rifle shots only a few feet away. His back was to the gun, too.

Nerves on his neck prickled, crawled as he thought how he had stood there, striking matches, with, a gun covering him all the time. He could have been shot down easier than Jump-John.

"All right," Mike said without looking around. "Now what?"

"Drop the reins. Step back with your hands in the air."

Mike took two steps back, grinning mirthlessly. It had been hard to believe his ears, but now there was no doubt that a woman held the gun on him.

"Drop your gun," she ordered. Her voice was thin, tight, unsteady. Clear, though. Any other time it might have been a pretty voice.

"Supposing I don't?" Mike said, listening for sign of a man. But if there were a man, he would have done the talking.

"I don't want to shoot you like a dog." She sounded close to tears, as if nerves were ragged and tight, and her unsteady finger might press the trigger any instant. And she added: "Shooting is too good for you. They'll know how to settle you in Salt Fork."

"Here goes the gun," Mike said. The moonlight still flooded on him. The soft thud of the gun on the mat of pine needles was audible.

"Now step back away from it."

Mike stepped back without trying to look around. "Mind telling me, ma'am, how come you're out here by Black Butte this time of evening? It ain't a place for a woman."

"If I hadn't met his horse heading back home and followed up the back trail, I wouldn't have caught you robbing his body. The rope they'll put around your neck will be too good for you."

She must have been standing just beyond the pine trunk all

the time he'd been examining the body, Mike thought. Not half a dozen steps away. One easy shot would have finished him—and she'd been in the mind to do it.

"Lady," Mike said over his shoulder, "I don't rob dead men. Ain't you a little hasty about a rope around my neck?"

The damp pine needles were almost noiseless under her movements. The rifle muzzle was prodding Mike's back before he knew she had come out from behind the pine. Her voice was bitter, scornful.

"You sneaking thief. I saw you take his money belt. And you knew where he was. I saw you come along the trail, looking for him. One of your friends must have shot him, and you came back to rob him."

Mike whistled softly. "So that's how you got it figured? He your husband?"

"I haven't any husband. He's my brother." She jabbed fiercely with the rifle. "You hear me? *My brother!* Shooting's too good for you. Hanging's too good for a miserable thief like you."

"Sister, huh?" Mike said, and his voice hardened as he thought of old Jump-John. "I might've known. Bushwhacking's more in the family line, ain't it?"

"What do you mean?" Somehow a little of the anger was gone as she put the question.

"You ought to know if you've grown up a sister to him," Mike said harshly. "Don't tell me you don't know he was a skunk. A man doesn't get his age an' turn bushwhacker in a day. He's killed his men and run a dirty trail before, an' the family must have known it. He got what was coming to him . . . an', if there's any more like him in the family, they'll probably end up the same way. Get that gun out of my back. I don't hurt women."

The rifle muzzle stayed hard in his back. But her voice changed to huskiness, to something close to fright. "Who are you? What are you talking about?"

"Mike McBride, from the Circle Eight. I rode here from our beef drive to Two Rivers. One of our men was coming from Salt Fork to meet us when your brother bushwhacked him here. Old Jump-John killed him an' managed to find us an' tell us before he died. I wasn't robbing the body. I took the money belt to give to the Salt Fork sheriff. Your brother asked for what he got. Killing me won't help. The Circle Eight men know about it."

"So that's what happened?"

"That's what happened," Mike said harshly.

"I . . . I believe you."

"Thanks," Mike said ironically over his shoulder.

"D-don't take that belt to the sheriff," she pleaded.

"I'll take it if I can get there, lady," Mike promised grimly.

"Stand still. Don't try to f-follow me," she gulped. She was crying in soft, racking sobs that she seemed to be trying to conceal.

Despite the grim memory of Jump-John, Mike's anger vanished. This woman sounded young and suddenly helpless in grief and hurt. The gun left his back and she was gone.

Mike swung around and glimpsed her running out of the moonlight into the dark shadows beyond the pine, back toward the horse that had nickered. She stumbled slightly as her foot slipped, and kept on, a slim, small figure with both hands still clutching the rifle.

The whispering sound of her sobs came back for a moment, and then she was indistinct and vanishing in the night shadows.

A dead stick cracked, her horse nickered again, and then the stamp of hoofs, the crackling of branches, marked her spurring retreat on the horse.

Mike stood there, alone with the dead man. He could have followed her—and perhaps been shot at. A woman in her state might do anything.

61

Helpless and crying, trying only to get away from him. As if he were guilty of her hurt. He didn't know who she was, but he was sure now that she hadn't realized the dead man was a killer. And she'd believed Mike McBride's angry words without question. Believed and fled.

"Didn't even give me an argument," Mike muttered, scowling down at the dead man.

But the dead couldn't hear or answer back, and the girl was gone. It would be hard and maybe dangerous to try to catch her.

She must live this side of Salt Fork. It wouldn't be hard now to find out who the dead man was. And, meanwhile, Concho Walker was in Salt Fork, maybe in trouble.

Mike left the dead man there under the big pine and started on toward Salt Fork. And the bleak, cold anger at Jump-John's killer was grimmer now, and he couldn't get his mind off that sobbing, fleeing girl.

IV

Salt Fork was a raw, new town that had mushroomed at the fork of Salt Creek and Blue River. When, years ago, old Concho had brought his mortgaged cattle onto the lush grass north of the Screwjack Hills, Salt Fork had been only a few shanties and a trading post.

When the button named Mike McBride had thrown in with the Circle 8, the last Indian outbreak had just been cleaned up to the west, gold had been discovered in the Cohita Mountains, a hundred and fifty miles farther west, and the easiest way for the freight was through Salt Fork. With the Indians out of the way, cattle were safe in the Screwjack country and the settlers had come fast.

Salt Fork had grown as fast and been made the seat of a new country. And on his Circle 8 land Concho had grumbled about the rush of strangers that put neighbors within ten or fifteen miles and made Salt Fork, a bare fifty miles away, a raw, wide-open cattle town almost under their noses.

It was an hour's fast ride from the Black Butte to Salt Fork. The claybank was foam-flecked and blowing hard when Mike dismounted before the Colorado House, the two-story adobe hotel where the stages stopped.

Wagons and horses were at the hitch racks along the muddy street. Windows were lighted, indicating that Salt Fork was wide awake. Mike walked stiffly into the hotel and spoke to a fat, gloomy-looking clerk who was seated on a high stool behind the counter, making entries in a ledger.

"Where can I find a gent by the name of Concho Walker?" Mike demanded.

The fat man started and spilled a drop of ink on the sheet as he looked up and blinked. "You mean the old man who owns the Circle Eight?"

"That's him? Is he around?"

"He's been around," the fat man said sourly. His pen tip indicated the long rafters behind Mike. "Peel your eye up there, bub, an' you'll see where he shot hell out o' the ceiling this afternoon. Said he was goin' to write his son's name up there so Salt Fork'd never forget it. He like to shot the shirt tail oft a preacher that had the room up there."

"I ain't 'bub' and the preacher can look after his own shirt tail," Mike said coldly. "What's the son's name?"

"Walker, I reckon. That's the old 'un's name."

"He have the son with him?"

"Not as I seen."

"Where's Walker now?"

"The devil only knows," the fat man said sourly. "I only hope he stays away until he sobers up."

Several men sitting in chairs had listened to the conversation.

One of them said: "He was at the Gold Rush a couple of hours ago, going strong. Drinks is free, an' he swears he'll have the whole town drunk tonight."

"Why doesn't the sheriff lock him up?" Mike demanded harshly.

"If Ban Shelton locked up everyone that bought drinks fer the town," the fat clerk grumbled, "Salt Fork'd be a hell of a place. Shelton's got the right idea. He lets 'em have a good time."

"Specially when they howdy-do as how they'll pin a few ears back with a stud deck as soon as they square off at a table with any gents who'd like to learn poker from an expert," the other man drawled. "Shelton ain't the man to annoy his gambler friends by lockin' the sucker up, is he?"

A queer look came over the clerk's fat face.

"That ain't no way to be talkin'. Shelton wouldn't like it."

"I'll bet not," the speaker agreed in his lazy drawl.

He was a clean-shaven, middle-aged man in a black suit, gray hat, and expensive half boots. His air of prosperity suggested that he came from one of the larger towns. Long slim hands unmarked by hard work hinted that he might be a gambler. But his lip had curled with disdain when he spoke of the sheriff's gambler friends.

The clerk cleared his throat, frowned, and started to say something. Then he pressed his lips together, dipped the pen into the ink, and hunched back over his ledger.

"Thanks," Mike said, and hurried out.

At least Concho hadn't gotten himself into a gunfight. But old Jump-John had been right. Concho was on a hellacious drunk that might lose him the Circle 8 and everything he had built up in the lean hard years of his old age.

Larrupin' Ed had called the turn, too. Concho had dried out too long. And now the old man was roaring wild on whiskey, at the mercy of any crooked gambler who might be friendly with the sheriff. Mike was scowling as he looked in a saloon, saw no customers, and crossed the muddy street toward another saloon.

Ban Shelton, Salt Fork's sheriff, had been in office less than a year. Mike had seen him only once, from across the street, a tall, stringy man with a reddish mustache, a fancy, pearl-handled revolver, and a big, fancy white sombrero.

Shelton was a Texas man. He was said to be handy with a gun, and was backed by all the Texicans who had settled in the south part of the county.

The second saloon had only one customer and he was not Concho. Mike studied the hitch racks and building fronts along the street for signs of the most life, and ended up at a low adobe building that housed the Stag Saloon.

The Stag hitch rack was crowded with horses. Loud voices, laughter, fiddle and piano music were audible inside. And as Mike walked in, a high-pitched Rebel yell keened over the other sounds.

A burst of laughter followed. The tall, gaunt bearded man in a battered black hat and worn buckskin who had given the yell sighted Mike and took a step toward him, whooping: "Mother, a stranger! An' walkin' steady an' sober er my name ain't Jubal Lark! What'll it be, young feller? You cain't stay the only sober 'un in town!"

Mike grinned as he allowed himself to be urged to the bar.

"Whiskey," Mike said. "I hear Concho Walker's getting the town drunk."

Jubal Lark whooped again. "Concho Walker! *There's* a man who'll do fer ary partner. Knowed him on the Picket Wire thirty year ago, I did, an' they wa'n't ary currycomb made fer him then. We're a-drinkin' to Concho's boy, an' I'm keepin' 'er pourin' while Concho gits him some rest with a leetle poker. Barkeep! Everybody's drinkin'! I got the dust to pay fer it!

Gold's gold in ary place you see hit. An' I got the gold." His Rebel yell split the noise again. "Drink up on Jubal Lark an' Concho Walker! Hit's free an' hit's here a-waitin'!"

Whoops and yells marked the rush to the already crowded bar. The crowd was good-naturedly noisy and drunk.

It must have been going on for hours. Mike had never seen anything like it. Concho had liquored up most of Salt Fork. Half a dozen men already were lying helplessly against the walls where they had been dragged.

"Where'd you say Concho was?" Mike asked Jubal Lark.

"In the back, havin' him a few cyards. You know Concho, young feller?"

Mike nodded.

Jubal Lark dropped an arm on his shoulder and grabbed for his hand.

"I'm proud to know you, son. Concho's friends is Jubal Lark's friends. Git outside that drink an' I'll take you to Concho. He's a-waitin' fer you, boy. Concho's a-waitin' fer all his friends. We'll tote him a bottle an' bring him luck with them cyards."

The drink helped after the wet day and hard ride. But Mike was hard-eyed and watchful as he edged away from the bar after Jubal Lark.

V

The saloon was L-shaped, with the bar in front and the side of the L a long, beamed, room holding a dance floor and tables. Jubal Lark wove toward a door in a partition at the back.

A man drinking beer at a table near the door stood up when Mike and Jubal Lark approached. The big, white sombrero topping the tall, stringy figure was familiar before Mike recognized Ban Shelton, the sheriff.

Shelton hitched his gun belt up as he stepped over before the door. "Where you men headin'?" he demanded.

"Bringin' luck an' a friend to my ole pard, Concho!" Jubal Lark whooped. "Step in with us, Sheriff, an' clean out your guzzle with some real drinkin'. Beer ain't ary way to be celebratin' with Concho."

The sheriff blocked the way.

"I'm drinkin' what I like, an' the boys in there are doin' what they like. They don't want to be bothered. You men wait at the bar. They'll be out when they get ready."

"Ain't a time when Concho wa'n't ready to see his old pard, Jubal Lark. He's a-dryin' an' a-thirstin' fer this bottle we're bringin' him."

"You ain't bringin' him anything," Shelton snapped with a quick loss of patience. "I'm keepin' order around here, an', if the boys say they don't want to be bothered, I'll keep it that way for them while I'm around. Go on back to the bar like I'm tellin' you. 1 don't want to lock you up!"

"Ain't anybody gonna lock Jubal Lark up fer tryin' to see an old pardner."

Ban Shelton's weathered, reddish face was long and angular, with a small, tight mouth. And the mouth was hard now as he bit out: "I'll lock you up so damn' quick you won't know what happened, old-timer. Don't crowd me, even if you *are* feelin' good."

"Wait a minute," Mike said, elbowing Jubal aside. "Nobody's breaking any law by walking in on a card game to speak to a man. Since when did the Salt Fork sheriff start watching the door for a poker game?"

Ban Shelton's angular face reddened.

"Zippy young squirt, ain't you? Who'n hell are *you?*"

"McBride's the name. I work for the Circle Eight brand. I rode here to see Concho Walker, and I aim to see him. Anything in your law book that says I can't see him?"

Ban Shelton's eyes were set close and mean-looking when

you watched them narrowing and flaming in dislike, as they did now.

"My law book says you're too damn' smart for your age," he said harshly. "It's got six pages, a handle, an' a steel barrel. An' I'll bend it over that swelled young head if you don't get back to the bar with this man an' stop disturbin' the peace. That's final warnin'."

Mike was grinning. He'd grinned like this before, and felt like this inside when the wild fracas had started in the El Paso saloon. It was a hot and surging feeling inside, like fire suddenly roaring up against trouble.

"Working with the tinhorn gamblers, are you?" he said, still grinning. "Get those hands up. Turn around. Open that door."

Ban Shelton's look had turned venomous as the first words came out. His hand had slapped down toward the fancy, pearl-handled gun, but it stopped when he saw the fast outflip of Mike's old wooden-handled .45.

The sheriff's jaw stayed loose in amazement as Mike bit out the orders with the same cold grin. Slowly Shelton turned and reached for the doorknob. Mike jerked the pearl-handled six-gun from the holster.

Jubal Lark had sobered into quick uneasiness.

"Wait a minute, young feller," he protested. "They ain't no use stickin' up the sheriff. Trouble ain't Concho's idee today."

"Pick out a spot of floor an' guzzle yourself blind," Mike said through his teeth. "I'm handlin' this. You, Sheriff, hurry up. Let me see Concho Walker. I'm in a hurry."

"There'll be hell to pay for this," Ban Shelton threatened thickly as he stepped through the doorway into a dim passage beyond.

"Ask for it and you'll get it," Mike said. "Open up that card game an' show me Concho."

The edges of the second door on the right oozed light, and

murmuring voices. Then the bright-yellow lamplight glowed into the passage and the voices went silent as Shelton opened the door and stood there with his hands up.

"What the hell?" a nasal voice exclaimed.

Past the sheriff's shoulder, Mike saw a bottle, glasses, and cards on a table under a hanging brass lamp that was wreathed in bluish tobacco smoke.

A stud game by the lay of the cards. Four players. Concho had his back to the door. The nasal-voiced man was across the table, facing the door. Under the down-pulled brim of his hat, a lean, furrowed face eyed the sheriff fixedly.

On the right side of the table a burly, red-faced man with his vest open and his sleeves rolled up on big hairy arms had been dealing cards. He put the deck down slowly as his head turned on a thick, powerful neck. Under bushy black brows, his eyes narrowed at the doorway.

The fourth man, on the left side of the table, was small, lean, and young. Behind a scanty blond mustache his rather handsome face was suddenly nervous as he leaned forward and saw the sheriff. A stack of chips clattered softly as he dropped them on the table. He slid lower in the chair, as if shrinking from trouble.

"Get up, Concho!" Mike said sharply. "I've come for you!"

"Eh?" Concho's voice was thick. His chair scraped back and he staggered as he started to get up. "Who is it?"

"A damn' stranger lookin' for trouble on account of the old man," Shelton said harshly. "He drawed a gun on me."

"Shut up," Mike said. "Concho, come out of there!"

Concho caught at the chair to steady himself and lurched around into the doorway, peering to see what was happening. His stooped, spare frame hid the rest of the room for the moment. And back of Concho there was no warning as a gunshot blasted out the overhead light.

Mike couldn't shoot the sheriff in the back, but any tenderfoot would have recognized this as a mess of trouble for Mike McBride and Concho Walker.

"Damn your dirty tricks!" Mike swore as he jerked up the .45 to pistol-whip the sheriff out of the way.

The blow glanced off a shoulder. Shelton had nimbly dodged aside in the sudden dark as the pressure of the gun left his back.

"Duck, Concho!" Mike yelled. A second blasting shot in the card room drowned the words. Then there was a third shot.

A man lurched out of the doorway into Mike and would have fallen if Mike hadn't thrown out a supporting arm. It was Concho, reeking of whiskey and now worse than drunk.

Mike jumped back with Concho's sagging weight fully on his arm. He fired past Concho at a gun flash inside the card room doorway.

Concho was muttering something, but the words were lost as other guns hammered a hail of lead out the card room doorway. Bullets that would have riddled them both if Mike hadn't moved fast.

There was no time now to hear what Concho was saying. Concho was badly hit. He'd be killed and Mike McBride, too, if those poker sharks had their way.

VI

Mike bumped into Jubal Lark as he backed with Concho's stumbling weight. He was throwing shots past Concho at the doorway where red gun flashes searched after them. The sheriff had disappeared back in the dark hallway.

"Get outta the way!" Mike yelled, crowding back past Jubal Lark with his burden.

The numbing slam of a bullet furrowed his left arm, the arm that was holding up Concho. Maybe it meant another wound for Concho. The old man had been hit more than once. His weight was getting heavier.

Mike was raging with wild anger. This was like the killing of old Jump-John. This was cold murder a second time, without any excuse or reason that a man could see. Murder backed by Ban Shelton, the sheriff.

Concho was stumbling badly, ready to fall. There wasn't a chance to duck for cover and make a stand. Mike's shoulder hit the side of the doorway. He staggered back out of the passage, found the open door with a sweep of his arm, and slammed it shut.

Beside him, Jubal Lark grumbled: "Why'd you have to start trouble thataway, young 'un? What's the matter with Concho?"

Concho's knees buckled and a great groan wrenched from him. "Can't make it any more, Mike," he gasped. "Lemme down an' run fer it."

Here, outside the passage, there was dim light from the front of the saloon. Light that showed Concho's weathered, wrinkled face contorted with pain.

Blood was spreading over Concho's shoulder. A great red blotch was widening on the front of his shirt. Mike swallowed a groan as he saw that a bullet had gone in Concho's back and torn out big in the front. Concho didn't have a chance.

Concho knew it. His look had cleared and steadied. Concho was a sober man now, calling on the last of his strength as he tried to push Mike away.

"Jubal," Concho gasped.

"Here, pardner."

"Help the boy git away. He's my boy. My son. Don't let 'em git him."

"Hell's blazes, whyn't somebody say so?" Jubal Lark blurted. "He never told me. Shore I'll watch him."

Jubal Lark whirled menacingly toward the crowd that was

cautiously moving out from the bar into the other end of the L-shaped room.

"Git back there!" Jubal Lark yelled. "Keep out o' this! I'll plug the first snake that gits in our way!"

Concho was sitting on the floor now, supporting himself with a hand as Mike finished reloading the .45 and cocked the sheriff's fancy revolver in the other hand.

"Where's your real son?" Mike asked huskily. "I'll get to him if I can an' tell him."

"Always wanted a son," Concho wrenched out. "Been aimin' fer it since you throwed in with me, Mike. I come here to Salt Fork this trip an' made it legal. Lawyer Sanders drawed up the papers so you'll git the Circle Eight an' all I own. I took me a drink to celebrate . . . an' couldn't stop the celebratin'." Concho gulped and smiled faintly. "Ain't every day a old hard shell like me gits a bang-up son he's so proud about."

Mike's throat was suddenly tight, so that it was hard to speak. His eyes were moistening strangely as he kneeled there on the rough floor with cocked six-guns and looked at Concho's lean, wrinkled face and bowed shoulders.

Concho's faded frosty eyes were clouding now, and yet they were bright, too, with a pride and satisfaction Mike had never before seen.

"You needn't have done it," Mike gulped. "You've been better'n a father."

"Might 'a' whaled you a few times when I didn't," Concho said thickly, and managed to smile as he bowed there with a hand over the torn hole in his stomach and blood creeping out over the gnarled fingers.

A spasm passed over Concho's face. He fought it away and gasped: "Listen while I can talk. It's the only chance I'll get to talk to a real son. You've growed up now. I want you to keep growin'. Don't wait like me till you're busted down an' wore out afore you git your roots in an' start growin'. You're young. You can go a long way with the start you got. Savvy?"

"Sure, Concho."

"Savvy this, then," Concho gasped. "I aim fer you to keep growin' head an' shoulders over ary man you ever knowed. Listen, boy. I'm dyin'. I can't be with you like I counted on. I aim fer you to end up a king cowman that men'll talk about from Saint Louie to Frisco. I aim fer you to do all the things I should've done an' be all the things I might've been. You listenin', son?"

Jubal Lark was stamping back and forth beside them, warning the saloon crowd away. The sheriff and gamblers hadn't appeared. They might any second. Concho's eyes were clouding fast. Mike didn't know where he was getting the strength to hold himself up and pour out the dry, feverish words.

Kneeling there with the two .45s cocked and ready for the gunfight that might resume any second, Mike nodded again, unashamed tears in his eyes.

"I'm listening, Concho. I won't forget."

"You're young enough to make it," Concho said. "It'll mean your heart an' your head'll have to keep growin with your bank account. Jealous men'll try to cut you down. Some that seem friends'll try to double-cross you. You'll have to be hard an' soft at the right time, an' sharp *all* the time. Your feet'll have to stay hard on the ground while you're lookin' up above where you're climbin'. An' when you get there, son, I want you to be proud an' big, with no shame behind you. Savvy?"

"I savvy, Concho . . . all of it!"

Concho was looking at him, but the faded eyes had a faraway look, as if Concho already were leaving and straining back for a last look.

Concho's voice was fading away, too.

"No matter where you bury me, son, I'll be lookin' when you

git up there to the top. I'll be proud I pointed you right . . . proud of ol' Concho Walker's son. . . ."

"Concho!" Mike caught the collapsing figure and eased it to the floor. Concho's eyes had closed. He was past hearing now, past caring what happened to Concho Walker. He had gone far and was going faster, farther each moment.

"He's dying," Mike gulped.

"Like he wanted to," Jubal Lark jerked out. "Concho use to say he'd like to git it with his boots on an' guns smokin' close. Ain't no more we can do, boy. Our skins is next. Let's get outta here."

Mike stood up, blinking, gripping the two cocked six-guns. There was no time now to think it all out. There, at his feet, Concho was dying. One of the gamblers had shot Concho in the back. And savagely Mike knew what had to be done.

"Ride your trail!" Mike threw at Jubal Lark as he turned toward the passage door.

"What you doin'?"

"I'm getting the dirty son-of-a-bitch that killed Concho."

"No, you don't," Jubal Lark said decisively. "You're Concho's boy. I told him I'd git you outta here. That sheriff'll be back to even up the way you handled him."

But Mike elbowed past the older man, jerked open the door, plunged into the passage, taut and ready to meet triggered guns.

But the dark passage was quiet, deserted. The card room held no sign of life. On to the back Mike ran, guns cocked for any movement ahead. Then suddenly through another door he came out back of the building into the open night.

Jubal Lark was at his heels, protesting.

"They hightailed to a hole somewheres. You won't find 'em if you hunt all night. Git outta town, boy. That sheriff'll have help by now. You cain't gunfight him an' his friends all alone an' come out with your hair. Where's your hoss?"

74

"In front of the hotel," Mike muttered, peering about, listening.

Jubal Lark caught his arm and spoke with hoarse urgency.

"My hoss is at the feed barn. I'll git him an' meet you outta town on the Drippin' Springs trail. We'll jine your outfit an' talk things over. You'll do a heap more with friends at your back an' plans made than a-chargin' around in another man's town at night askin' for trouble. You go an' kill two, three o' them an' there'll be a dozen more to git you. *That* ain't what Concho figgered."

It was only words strung together, words that had no meaning for Mike McBride. Anger, grief at Concho's death had brought that cold, savage, wolfish feeling. They wanted gunfighting. They'd get gunfighting.

"Go get your horse," Mike said. "Don't worry about me."

Jubal Lark held onto his arm.

"Still want trouble, don't you? Cain't ride away an' leave hit to another day. You young hotheads is all the same. Listen, you're Concho's boy. You made Concho a dyin' promise. Are you gonna keep it?"

The harsh reminder struck Mike like cold water. It was as though Concho were standing there in the dark with the weight of his gnarled hand beside Jubal Lark's hand.

Mike wavered, surrendered. "Meet you out on the trail."

"Good boy. Keep offen the street till you get to the hotel an' then ride like hell. That blasted sheriff is wantin' you. He ain't forgot how you handled him."

Jubal Lark vanished in the night. Startled, Mike tried to follow the buckskin-clad man's retreat. He heard nothing, saw nothing. Jubal Lark had gone like a ghost. With a grunt of approval, Mike went the other way, cutting back behind the store buildings.

The crowd in the Stag Saloon was boiling out into the street.

The gun play, the dead man, the threat of more to come had silenced all but the noisiest ones.

Mike heard a few uncertain yells as he ran toward the hotel. He met no one back there in the dark behind the store buildings. Everything seemed quiet in front of the hotel. The claybank drooped at the hitch rail.

But as Mike holstered his gun and stepped out to the rack, a quiet voice said: "Trouble down the street there?"

Mike spun toward the voice, pulling his gun. Then he shoved it back into the holster as he recognized the clean-shaven stranger in the black suit and expensive boots who had spoken up in the hotel lobby. The man was leaning against the building front now, smoking a cigarette.

"I met the sheriff an' his friends," Mike said briefly as he turned back to the claybank and unwrapped the reins.

"Figured you might," the stranger drawled without moving. "Who got hurt?"

"The man I was looking for," Mike answered harshly as he reached to the saddle. "Murdered. Shot in the back. Might help you to remember that. In the back."

"My memory," the stranger drawled, "is good." His cigarette end was glowing red as Mike reined the claybank out into the street.

Back at the Stag Saloon there was more noise now as the drunken crowd spread along the street. Back there, too, was Concho Walker and a score that Mike McBride would settle before he again slept easy at night.

The bitter bite of it was in his throat as he settled in the saddle to ride, and the drumming crash of gunshots across the street was the first warning that he was not getting out of Salt Fork without more trouble. The next instant the claybank was screaming, rearing high.

Half a dozen guns, at least, were spurting fire. The claybank was badly hit. High it reared—and came down loosely, pitching forward into the muddy street.

Mike kicked out of the stirrups, threw himself clear of the saddle, hit the ground staggering, and sprawled in the mud. The six-gun he had drawn went deep into the mud, clogging the barrel.

Mike hurled the gun away as he scrambled up and clawed out the sheriff's gun that was thrust inside his belt. The shots had stopped as the horse went down; now they started again as Mike came up in the street.

A trip-hammer blow seemed to tear off the top of his head, and he felt himself falling into blackness that had no bottom.

VII

There was lamplight and men were about Mike. He was on his back, his shirt off. Someone was working on his arm.

The first words he heard sounded far away. His clearing head brought the voice suddenly just above him, speaking in a mild drawl.

"He was lucky. An eighth of an inch lower would have split his skull like a meat axe. This arm won't bother him much. It gouged out a little muscle and he lost some blood. But he's young and husky enough to stand it."

"He'd be better off if he'd leaked all his blood," an angry voice broke in. "Because I'm gonna hang him an' laugh while the rope stretches his dirty neck. I'd have killed him back there in the street if I'd known about him then."

"He's your prisoner now. Better not lose your head," the mild voice advised. "After all, there might be a mistake."

"Mistake, hell. Witnesses seen him shoot old man Walker. That money belt in his saddlebag is one I give my brother. He had to kill Jake to get it. You tryin' to tell me he ain't a dirty killer?"

"I'm not trying to tell you he's anything," the mild voice said. "A jury will do that. But dead brother or not, Shelton, you'll do well to make sure he faces a jury. I'm telling you now that he'll be all right in a little while. I suggest you keep him that way."

"I'll ask for your advice when I want it," Shelton snapped. "Too damn' many folks tonight are tellin' me how I ought to act as a sheriff!"

The mild voice said: "I voted for you, Shelton. It was my understanding Salt Fork wanted a sheriff, not a judge, jury, and public executioner as you see fit. You'd have killed this man instead of arresting him as he lay there in the street if that stranger hadn't stopped you."

"A damned lone-wolf gambler buttin' into something that was none of his business. He's another 'un that'll learn to mind his own business."

"Shelton," the mild-voiced man said, "I'm a voter, a taxpayer, and the only medical man in three days' ride. You might remember that. A sheriff can always be replaced. A doctor can't."

The sheriff growled something as Mike opened his eyes. The doctor was putting on his black hat, barely past thirty by his looks, clean-shaven, with a thin, likable face.

Ban Shelton was there and another man, and behind them were jail bars. Mike lifted his head. He was on a cell cot. Half a dozen men beyond the bars had been watching the doctor work.

One of them exclaimed: "Looks like you was right, Doc! He's a-rearin' up."

"I'll handle him," Ban Shelton grunted. His red face was ugly as he said: "Where's Jake's body? Speak up or I'll choke it out of you!"

"Ask your sister," Mike said with an effort.

"What's Judy got to do with it?"

"She found the body. She'll tell you I took the money belt to bring to the sheriff. Not knowing you were brother to a man who'd bushwhacked an old man in cold blood."

"I don't know what in blazes you're talking about, McBride. It's a lie, whatever it is. Judy don't know Jake's dead or she'd have sent word. If you brought Jake's belt to the sheriff, why'n hell didn't you give it to me at the Stag instead of pulling a gun when I wasn't lookin' and crowdin' past to shoot that old soak you've been workin' for?"

Sitting on the cot edge, Mike was dizzy, sick with the hammering pain inside his bandaged head. The men outside the bars were watching for his reply. The doctor's look was thoughtful. Half an eye could see that even the doctor thought he'd shot Concho in the back.

Mike tried to stand up, protesting: "That's a lie. One of those gamblers shot Concho. One of your friends."

Shelton pushed him violently back on the cot. "That talk ain't helpin' you. There was witnesses. I saw it myself. We'll put you before a jury an' let them hang you. Now everybody clear out! I've got him safe and I'll keep him safe!"

"Just a moment," the doctor said. "What's this, Shelton, about your brother killing someone?"

"If this feller's got any kind of likely story he can tell it in court."

"Doc," Mike said, looking at the physician, "I need a lawyer. Tell Lawyer Sanders to get over here. The sheriff can't keep him out."

"That's right," the young doctor agreed. "I'll get Sanders at once."

"I don't hold a man from his legal rights," Shelton growled. "All right men, move on."

The sheriff locked the cell door. Alone, Mike hunched on the cot, holding his throbbing head.

Concho dead. Ban Shelton's brother dead. He, Mike McBride, charged with both killings. The money belt pinning one murder on him. Shelton and the gamblers swearing the other murder on him. Shelton knew it was a lie, knew who killed Concho.

Thinking back, it was easy to believe that Shelton must have known Concho didn't have a chance. And just now Shelton had stopped all questions about his brother, hustled witnesses out of the way. There was more to this than a card game and a killing, if a man could read the sign right.

Facts were plain. Concho had started his roaring drunk. Old Jump-John had taken Concho's horse and ridden to meet the Circle 8 drive.

Jake Shelton, the sheriff's brother, had shot Jump-John at the Black Butte. Jake Shelton must have followed Jump-John out of Salt Fork to stop him. And had almost done so. Almost left Concho drunk, helpless in the hands of the gamblers and Ban Shelton.

They couldn't have planned to kill Concho and lay the murder on Mike McBride, because they hadn't known Mike McBride was coming.

But while Concho was dying, Ban Shelton had made no attempt to reënter the Stag Saloon and arrest the man he was now charging with the killing. Shelton had gone for friends, had opened fire without warning as his man was riding away.

By the doctor's word, Mike McBride would have been killed there in the muddy street if a stranger hadn't stepped in.

All that had happened before Ban Shelton had found his brother's money belt in Mike McBride's saddlebag. Before Shelton knew that his brother was dead. For some reason Shelton had wanted Mike McBride as quickly dead as Concho.

You could bet good gold that Shelton still felt the same way, and not because of his brother. And then you could wonder why.

The girl'd know Mike thought to himself. *She said not to take*

the belt to the sheriff. She knew damned well her brother Jake got
what was coming to him. Knew her sheriff brother was up to
something snaky.*

VIII

Ban Shelton stepped back into the cell room alone. The fancy
pearl-handled six-gun was in his holster once more. He was
scowling as he spoke through the bars. "So Jake's dead?"

"Shot by the man he rode out of town to kill," Mike said.

"You're claiming another man killed Jake?"

"It was Jump-John Myers, who rode in here to Salt Fork with
Concho. Maybe you wouldn't be knowing that."

"Where's this Myers now?" Shelton demanded.

"Like to have a try at shutting his mouth, wouldn't you? Go
talk to your sister. She found your brother's body before I did.
She heard me say I was bringing the money belt in to the
sheriff."

"What did Judy say?"

"Ask her."

Shelton's blustering anger was under control now. His mouth
was tight and hard, eyes sharp, wary. He stared through the
bars as if trying to read the prisoner's face. A slow grin twisted
his mouth.

"You brought Judy into this. If you're lucky enough to get
into court, she'll help hang you."

"Wouldn't surprise me," Mike agreed. "It must run in the
family."

Someone entered the front office, and Shelton turned away.

Mike heard voices murmuring for several moments, then
Shelton brought in a smiling, roly-poly little man in a black
frock coat, black hat, and red cardboard note case under an
arm.

"Here's your lawyer," Shelton said curtly as he unlocked the

81

cell door. "He's a killer, Sanders, and it'll take a better man than you to get him out."

The lawyer chuckled, bringing little creases over his smooth pink cheeks. He looked plump, jolly, sure of himself.

"We'll let the law settle that, Sheriff. Lock the door and leave us alone."

"You bet I'll lock it. An' don't take all night. I'm leavin' with a posse to find Jake's body. I want you out o' here before I'm gone."

"According to the law. . . ."

Shelton cut him off brusquely. "Damn the law. I'm runnin' the jail tonight, Sanders, an' I'm in a hurry."

When they were alone in the cell, Mike indicated the other end of the cot for the lawyer to sit on and spoke grimly. "Shelton seems to be the sheriff an' the law both around Salt Fork."

"Talk. Only talk," the pink-checked little man said cheerfully as he sat down. "Now, then, young man, can you pay for a good lawyer?"

"Worried about the money already?"

"Lawyers have to live," Sanders reminded shrewdly.

"I reckon I can pay. Maybe you didn't get the name. I'm Mike McBride."

Sanders nodded. "Work for the Circle Eight, I understand."

"I reckon I own it now."

"*Hm-m-m.* Didn't this Concho Walker own the Circle Eight?"

"Concho signed papers making me his legal son. Said so in the Stag tonight just before he died. He told me to see you about it."

"You don't have to worry, then," Sanders said with returning cheerfulness. "Where are the papers?"

"You made 'em out," Mike said. "Where are they?"

"Eh?"

"Concho signed 'em."

Sanders stood up, smiling regretfully. "Walker did say something about drawing up some papers before he left town. Perhaps tomorrow. He didn't sign anything. If that's all the title you have to the ranch, young man, you haven't anything."

The little good-humored crinkles in the plump, smooth face were still there, but Mike suddenly realized that the smile held no friendliness. It was a tricky smile.

"You're lying," Mike charged. "Concho did sign those papers."

"I didn't come here to be called a liar, young man. If you're going to get. . . ."

"Concho trusted you an' you turned snake soon as he was dead."

Sanders yelled with fright, tried to dodge in the cramped, narrow little cell as Mike came off the cot. Mike caught him by the throat, slammed him against the back wall, sinking fingers deep into the puffy neck.

The lawyer's face mottled as he clawed at the corded wrists, eyes began to bulge.

"Concho's dead, but I'll get the truth out of you," Mike panted. "What happened to those papers? What'd you do with them?"

Then, outside the cell, Ban Shelton was shouting: "What's the matter here? Leggo him, McBride! Leggo before I gut-shoot you!"

Mike yanked the struggling little lawyer around for a shield.

"Lead's what *he* needs! Shoot the hell out of him!"

Cursing, Ban Shelton unlocked the door and plunged in with his gun. Mike hurled the half-throttled little lawyer across the cell at him.

"Drag the little buzzard out of here before I break his neck. Tell him he ain't heard the last of this if I'm hung on every gallows from here to the border. I ain't the only friend Concho

Walker had. It'll take more than a greasy little lawyer to work the trick he's trying."

Shelton pulled the stumbling, choking man outside the cell, slammed the door, and locked it.

"You get a lawyer an' then try to kill him as soon as my back's turned. It'll take a lynching to settle you, an' the quicker the better. Come on, Sanders. I reckon you're through here."

Coughing, feeling his neck, Sanders scurried into the sheriff's office without looking back.

Breathing heavily, Mike dropped back on the cot. The bullet-furrowed arm was hurting. The head felt worse. Inside, too. For the first time he felt like a trapped animal. He swore thickly as he rolled a cigarette with unsteady fingers.

This afternoon he'd been Mike McBride, twenty-one, owning half of a prosperous beef drive. Tonight, for a little while, he'd been Mike McBride, Concho's adopted son, owning all the beef drive and the Circle 8, too. Now, here in the Salt Fork jail cell, he was Mike McBride, Circle 8 cowhand, pockets almost empty, and a hang rope staring him in the face.

Mike swore again. Concho *had* signed those papers. Drunk or sober, Concho had told the truth before he died. Which made sign that anyone could read.

Concho had come to Salt Fork, left his business with a crooked lawyer, and let whiskey make him a target for every sharper in town.

They'd worked fast. They'd gone after Concho's ranch and cattle. They'd shot Concho out of the picture. Now they had Mike McBride locked up and were ready to hang him. They'd have killed him tonight in front of the hotel if the stranger hadn't stopped them.

Mike paced the cell like a caged wildcat. Activity was audible in the sheriff's office. Finally it stopped. A lanky man with a drooping mustache and a deputy's star pinned on his vest stepped back to the cell and peered through the bars.

"Ban's rode out o' town, an' I'm in charge. Y'all set for the night?"

"Coffee'd help my head."

The deputy shifted chewing tobacco into the other cheek and grinned loosely.

"This ain't a hotel. You'll get coffee with breakfast if you ain't lynched by then. Uhn-huh, lynched. Heap of folks in these parts thought well of Jake Shelton. Us Texans stays next to one another."

"That lawyer, Sanders, from Texas, too?"

"Shore is."

"Can't all of you be from Texas."

The deputy grinned again. "The ol' Lone Star's a big 'un."

"Ain't big enough to hold all the crooks, skunks, and snakes I've run into tonight," Mike said. "That goes for you, too. Get out so I can rest my eyes."

The deputy snarled back through the bars: "You won't be so damned talky iffen they get a lynch rope on your neck. An' I ain't got no help to stop 'em if they're minded. Ease your damn' head with that." He stamped out. Mike started pacing again. Three steps one way, three the other.

Both Shelton and his deputy had spoken about a lynching. Miss out on killing a man when you arrested him, and a lynch rope would settle everything before he walked into court to tell his side.

Mike stopped as something tapped faintly on the window glass. It was the end of a branch tapping the glass. By standing on his toes, Mike could push the window up part way and reach through the bars.

"You in there, boy?"

That would be Jubal Lark, outside under the window, speaking guardedly.

IX

Mike moved the cot over under the window and stood on it. "Get me a gun," he called in a low voice.

"Comin' up already, son."

Jubal Lark had cut and trimmed a small tree branch. The heavier end poked up through the bars bearing a .45 tied on by a whang string. With the gun was a leather pouch holding extra cartridges.

"Soon as I heered the shootin' I knowed that polecat sheriff'd found you," Jubal Lark's hoarse whisper came up. "Time I got near the spot they had you they was askin' where I was. I had to keep out o' sight. Ain't a chance fer me to git in there an' git you. There's a crowd out front."

"Working up to a lynching?" Mike whispered back through the bars.

"You might as well know hit," Jubal Lark agreed. "The fools is drunk an' believin' you walked right in an' holed Concho in the back. Them gamblers an' the sheriff swore you did. They're all fer lynchin' the *hombre* who kilt the feller that was buyin' 'em drinks. Come mornin' they'll git some sense. Tonight there ain't no reasonin' with 'em."

"An' by morning I'll be lynched."

"Looks bad if you don't git outta there, boy. The sheriff rode outta town. Ain't nobody to stop 'em. A friend o' your'n named Monte Hill has tried to talk sense to 'em an' didn't git nowhere. He's bringin' a hoss back o' the jail here fer you. If you can bust out, we'll side you out o' town."

Jubal spat audibly. "If you cain't, we'll take a hand an' try to git you out. They won't string you up, boy, whilst Jubal Lark can work a gun. I done promised Concho. How's your head?"

"Good enough," Mike said. "Who's this Monte Hill?"

"Friend o' your'n. He run out from the hotel an' made sure you wasn't kilt when they had you down in the street. Backed 'em cold by swearin' he'd take on ary man who stopped a doctor from gittin' to you. Sent for the doc hisself."

"I'll be out to thank him," said Mike. "And I'll have to leave town fast. They're charging me with double murder. The lawyer says Concho didn't sign any papers today. They're after the Circle Eight, too. Somebody'll have papers saying that Concho gambled away everything."

"So that's how hit is."

"The lawyer's a fat little man named Sanders," Mike continued. "Might be if I could talk to him out of town there'd be a different story."

"Fat little lawyer named Sanders," Jubal Lark repeated out in the darkness under the jail window. "You ride out the Drippin' Springs trail an' find your beef drive, boy. I've toted in slicker game than fat little lawyers. You'll git your talk with him. Jubal Lark's a-promisin' hit. An' don't waste your time in there. Them drunken fools is a-gatherin' an' a-inchin' up to a lynchin'. I'm wishin' you luck."

"Thanks."

Jubal Lark evidently vanished quickly again, for he did not reply.

All chambers in the six-gun he had brought were loaded. Mike shoved it under his belt, closed the window, and moved the cot back. Then he pulled on his muddy coat and buttoned it over the gun. His hat had evidently been left in the muddy street.

The left arm was stiff and painful, but usable. His head was feeling better. From the moment the gun came through the window, strength and hope had come flooding back. One friend outside had been all he needed. He had two. Three, if you counted the young doctor. Mike McBride had a chance now.

For a moment Mike had the feeling that old Concho was close, watching, waiting for Mike McBride to fight out of this trouble and start for those heights which Concho had planned.

Men might die. Concho might be avenged. But there was more to it than that. More than a jail cell. More than revenge for Concho and smooth trickery. This was the first testing of Mike McBride, who one day had to be all those things that Concho Walker might have been. It had been a promise to a dying man.

Voices had been audible out front. Now, with the window closed, there were still snatches of sound, as ominous and distant as thunder warning of a storm to come.

The deputy had put up a window and was parlaying not very vigorously with someone. His office door opened, closed, and he talked to someone who had joined him.

If they got several more men in the office, there wouldn't be much chance to get out past them. Mike called until the deputy came back into the little cell corridor.

"Going to let them lynch me?" Mike demanded.

"I'll stop 'em if I can."

"More likely you'll follow along to pull on the rope."

The deputy's loose-lipped grin admitted it as he suggested: "Maybe you could talk 'em out of it from the front window. I'll iron your wrists an' give you the chance if you want it. They ain't listenin' to me."

"A sight of me will start 'em off," Mike reminded. "I'll be there in the office, ironed and cold meat to grab and drag outside."

"It's your only chance, McBride. I'll give ary prisoner his chance."

Mike grinned, too. He had that wolfish, savage feeling again.

"You and Ban Shelton," he said. "I'll try it."

The deputy was chuckling as he stepped back into the office, chuckling when he returned with wrist irons and the cell keys.

"Stick out your wrists an' oil up your tongue. They're waitin' to hear you, an' there's company in the office to swear you got a fair deal."

The office door had swung shut. Mike was grinning, too, as he put his left hand through the bars.

"Might be you'll have the same chance you're giving me," he said.

"Cain't tell, young feller." The deputy grinned.

Both his hands were bringing the iron to the wrist when Mike caught him and yanked him close to the .45 muzzle that the other hand had flipped out from under the coat.

"Quiet. Here's *your* chance now."

The deputy read death in the thin smile and gasped through the sudden terror on his face.

"Get the key in that lock."

The arm Mike held was trembling. The deputy was swallowing as if his throat had clogged. His shaking hand missed the keyhole twice before he unlocked the cell door.

Mike stepped out. "Want a chance to draw?" he invited.

"No, no. I ain't. . . ."

"Shut up, then."

A moment later the deputy was ironed by a wrist to one of the cell bars. While he watched the office door and swiftly buckled on the deputy's gun belt, Mike warned: "Keep quiet while I go out. Tell Shelton I'm saving you both the same chance you gave me."

The deputy nodded dumbly. Mike inspected both guns, thumbed the hammers, jerked open the office door, and stepped in. "Reach high and quiet," he said curtly.

Then he gasped. The office held only a startled girl who jumped up from a chair. She wore riding skirt and jacket, a silk handkerchief around her throat, and her yellow hair looked soft and wind-blown about her thin, startled face.

"I . . . I was looking for a man," Mike said lamely. "Keep

quiet an' you'll be all right."

Beyond drawn window shades, voices outside the jail were plainer. And the girl's reply was steadier than he expected.

"You're the one they want," she guessed swiftly.

She was small and slim, and her eyes were unhappy. And Mike would have known that clear note in her voice anywhere.

"You're Judy Shelton."

She nodded.

"Got here in a hurry to help hang me, didn't you? Must run in the family."

That brought a blaze into her eyes. He'd thought her young, but not so young. Not younger than himself. Looking now, it was hard to believe she'd held him up by the Black Butte as coolly as a man.

"I believed you about Jake's money belt," she said scornfully. "And you rode into town and killed the man who was hiring you."

"You know the straight of it," Mike threw at her. "You knew the truth out there tonight. Ban Shelton and his gambler friends did the killing tonight. Pity you ain't a third brother. I'd start on you. They voted for a sheriff last year an' got a buzzard. He made the law gun law." Mike lifted the .45. "I'm raising him with six-guns. Him an' his friends an' any more of the Shelton breed that's running a loop on this range."

A drunken yell split the night outside. "What're we waitin' for? Let's git him!"

Mike grinned mirthlessly. "That would sound good to your brother Ban. Better get in the back room. These windows won't stop lead." He turned the light out as he spoke.

And through the swift blackness that fell between them, Judy Shelton cried in protest: "They'll kill you! Brazos Jones is leading them. I . . . I saw him when I came in. There must be some other way. I . . . I'll help you."

"Never heard of Brazos Jones. And the Sheltons," Mike answered her bitterly, "have helped me enough. Get back out of the way. Hell'll be popping in a minute."

Mike opened the door. He was in blackness. Cloudy moonlight brushed shadowy pallor over the muddy street outside the jail. Enough light to see the gathering crowd, two score or more. Some hanging back beyond the hitch rack and spreading to right and left along the slippery plank walk. Most of them liquored up, by the noise they were making. And the leaders already close to the jail steps, bunching up behind a broad-shouldered, powerful man who had drawn a gun and shouted as the door opened.

"That's right, Tomkins! Open up! All we want is that young killer! Come out with your hands up an' you won't have any trouble!"

One quick look placed the men. There was enough light to mark the big fellow shouting at the doorway. He must be Brazos Jones. He was the burly, red-faced gambler with the bushy black brows and hairy arms who had been sitting at Concho's right hand in the back of the Stag Saloon. One of the men who'd murdered Concho.

Mike could have opened fire from the dark doorway and riddled Brazos Jones and some of the drunken men behind Jones. Dropped them before they broke into the jail. Scattered them in panic for a few moments. But if he did that, in years to come the dead men would haunt Mike McBride. Many of the drunks were convinced that the prisoner was a killer. Sober, they'd look at the dead who hadn't fired a shot, and swear that all charges against Mike McBride must be true.

Mike made an instant choice before he moved—and took the greater risk.

"Stand back! Don't shoot!" he yelled as he dived out of the dark doorway.

X

Uncertainty stopped even Brazos Jones while a man might count four. In that time Mike dodged to the right along the front of the jail, cocked guns silent, the hell of gunfire and death hanging by a thread.

Then a bawl of anger came from Jones: "That's McBride! Get him!"

The big gambler's gun crashed furiously at the shadowy figure plunging to the corner of the building. Three shots came almost as one while Mike gambled with death to reach that jail corner without killing a man. And maybe he was a fool and maybe not. Concho would know.

A foot slipped on the rain-soft ground as he ducked around the corner. He stumbled, found footing, and raced toward the back of the jail. Other guns had opened up. The lynch crowd was milling in excitement and uncertainty, some of them not sure yet what was happening.

Brazos Jones dashed around to the side of the jail. Mike spun around, saw the big figure, the red-spurting gun muzzle. The smile that bared his teeth was cold and hard as the two big .45s blasted and roared in his hands. The gambler and a man or two bolder than the rest were leading the wolf pack to kill. For years Mike McBride had been growing up for this moment. Music and a wild, surging excitement were in the six-guns that blasted and bucked in his hands. Head and wounded arm were forgotten. Screaming lead fanned death about him, and he had no thought for it as he triggered at the gambler's shadowy figure at the front of the building.

The men behind Brazos Jones and others on the plank walk out front dashed back and aside from the red gun muzzles that had suddenly turned on them.

Brazos Jones jumped into the shadows beside the jail building—and then lurched out, staggering a step or two as he fell.

"There he is, Concho!" Mike yelled. "Maybe he's the one!"

Excitement had him now like whiskey running fire in his blood. Gun law they wanted, and gun law they'd get. The man behind the jail must have yelled several times before Mike heard him.

"McBride, you fool! Fork this horse!"

Then Mike realized he'd been standing there, shouting for Brazos Jones and the others to come and get him. They'd given him open space clear out into the street, and Brazos Jones was huddled on the muddy ground where he had fallen.

The man behind the jail was in the saddle and leading another saddled horse. Mike made a flying jump, clawed into the saddle, found the stirrups, and grabbed for the reins as the man spurred away, yelling: "This way!"

Jubal Lark wasn't there. As he followed, Mike recognized the gray hat and black suit of the man he'd last seen in front of the hotel.

"Are you Monte Hill?" Mike called as he spurred alongside.

"Shut up and ride! They'll be after us! This way!"

Monte Hill galloped through an open lot away from the main street. Dogs ran, barking at them. They passed lighted windows and staring figures in open doorways. Then they were past the last houses and corrals, racing into the south.

"The old fellow said you'd go to Dripping Springs!" Monte Hill called.

"Our herd won't get that far tonight! Thanks for the help! I'll make it all right now!"

"I'm siding you! Pour it on!"

Miles out of town, east of the stage road, they reined up a second time. They were alone in the vast night.

"Lost 'em," Monte Hill decided.

"This makes a second favor I owe you," Mike said. "Are you

sure Jubal Lark didn't get hurt?"

"He had some business that'd keep him a while," said Monte Hill. "He'll be all right."

Miles farther on they crossed the Dripping Springs trail, Mike guiding, and rode south and east for the Salt Fork Crossing and Black Butte. Mike's thoughts turned back to Judy Shelton, young and anguished as she had again abruptly sided with him.

"Shelton's sister was at the jail," Mike said aloud.

Monte Hill nodded. "I saw her ride by the livery barn. By the looks of her horse, she'd come fast. Must have heard about her brother Jake."

"She found his body," Mike said. "I met her there when I got the money belt to bring to the sheriff."

"That the way you got it?"

Mike told him what had happened, from Jump-John's death to the lawyer's visit to the jail.

"I had an idea Shelton's story was wrong," Monte Hill said coolly. "Good riddance to Jake. So Dude Ringold, Parson Pitts, and Shelton are after your ranch?"

"Those first two names are new."

"Gamblers," Monte Hill said. "Dude Ringold's good-looking, with a light mustache. He'd rob his own mother. I hear that Parson Pitts was in the poker game, too. He's worse. They were friends of Shelton back in Texas."

"Know plenty about them, don't you?"

Monte Hill shrugged. "I've been through Texas. What do you aim to do now?"

"Maybe I'll have an idea by morning."

"You'd better," Monte Hill remarked. "Because Ban Shelton will have ideas tonight."

They were pushing the horses. By Monte Hill's watch it was past 1:30 A.M. when they forded the Salt Fork, miles south of

Black Butte. By 3:00 they sighted the wan glow of the Circle 8 wagon fire and hailed Gus Delight, riding night trick on the bedded steers.

Jump-John had been buried and the cattle thrown on a bed ground a mile or so away. Gus Delight was profane with dismayed anger as he rode with them to the sleeping men near the fire.

"Crawl out! Concho's dead! Git out, all of you, an' hear trouble!"

They came awake—Jim Crowder, Slim Chance, Sam Parks, Larrupin' Ed Shaw, Dozy, the cook, and Guaymas Red, the part-Mexican wrangler with red hair who'd rather use a knife than a gun.

And as fresh, damp wood sizzled on the fire, Guaymas Red was as bitter as the rest when Mike told what had happened.

Larrupin' Ed Shaw spoke the violent thought of every man.

"We'll ride in on them snakes. Damn, if I'd only gone along."

Monte Hill spoke coolly. "Ban Shelton's not there tonight. Half the town's still drunk enough to think McBride killed your boss. Better wait."

"You t'ink we do nothing for thees?" Guaymas Red said angrily.

"I'm waiting for this man, Jubal Lark," Mike said. "We'll want good horses ready, Red. Dozy, how about some coffee? The rest of you better sleep it out till daybreak."

But there was no sleeping. Gun belts and rifles were brought to the fire and checked. Hot coffee warmed them and questions were volleyed at Mike until all details were known.

"If that damned lawyer gets here, he'll talk," Larrupin' Ed harshly promised.

"He'll talk," Mike agreed, and noticed Monte Hill watching him reflectively. The man was younger than he'd seemed at first. And more of a mystery than ever.

The steers grazed out as the false dawn gave way to the first faint gray. Monte Hill had wrapped himself in a borrowed blanket and tarp, and slept near the fire. Mike moved stiffly about, thinking. Even now it was hard to believe that Concho was dead, that he was on his own now.

Jubal Lark hadn't appeared by the time Dozy called grub. The clouds were thinning. A scarlet sunrise colored the east. Monte Hill rolled out of his blanket and joined Mike.

"Time enough for that old fellow to be here."

"I don't like it," Mike admitted. "I should have stayed."

"They'd have hunted you down."

"That lawyer," said Mike, "was my only chance to show crooked work. I'm outlawed. Shelton'll make sure I'm hunted." Mike spoke savagely. "Killing Ban Shelton might make it worse. I'm through on this range, no matter what I do."

"Going to quit and run."

"What's it to you?" Mike said curtly.

Monte Hill was silent for a moment before he drawled: "Judy Shelton helped her brothers get away from stock detectives who were ready to send them to the pen. One of the detectives had been fool enough to tell her, hoping she'd understand what he had to do. She didn't tell her brothers he wasn't the gambler they thought he was. But after they were safely gone, Judy told the man she was through with him. She'd never marry anyone who might take her brothers to court. She'd never marry anyway and disgrace a husband with her brothers, she said. She was young and broken up, and she meant it. He had to leave. And a year later he came back. Judy's mother was dead of heartbreak, they said, and Judy had gone west to the Screwjack country. He came after her and found she'd joined her brothers and hadn't changed her mind. So he stayed around to see if the brothers wouldn't hang themselves by their own cussedness after folks found them out."

"And you're hoping this will do it," Mike guessed.

"Hoping like hell," Monte Hill drawled, "since I'm hog-tied and helpless because of Judy."

"I wondered about you," Mike admitted. "Maybe we'll both have luck."

They were eating when Dozy called from the grub wagon: "Who's a-comin'?"

Riders had topped the slope to the west—four riders loping toward the wagon. One man wore a white sombrero that brought Mike to his feet.

"That's Shelton, the sheriff," Mike said grimly.

XI

Larrupin' Ed picked up his rifle. "Sit tight, Mike. They ain't gonna get you."

Mike grinned coldly. "Meet him on the other side of the wagon. I'll keep out of sight for a minute."

Monte Hill joined Mike behind the wagon. "He's fast with a gun," he warned. "There's only three men with him, but he rode out of Salt Fork with nine or ten last night."

Mike looked past the wagon seat. "Ain't that the card sharp, Parson Pitts, with him?"

"And Lafe Cantwell and Montana Jack," said Monte Hill, looking. "They're killers."

Standing there behind the wagon, they heard Larrupin' Ed greet the newcomers.

"Howdy, gents."

"I'm Sheriff Shelton. Mister Pitts, here, took over the Circle Eight last night. I've seen the papers Walker signed, and you can deal with Pitts from now on."

"Concho Walker'll tell us that."

The gambler's nasal voice said: "Walker's dead. Shot by one of his own men named McBride. The sheriff's got McBride locked up in Salt Fork for trial. Walker lost his ranch in a card game before he was killed. You men can have your pay and move on this morning."

Gus Delight's voice exploded high and angrily.

"No tinhorn gambler that oughta get what this Jake Shelton got fires me from anywhere while I got a hawglaig to talk . . . !"

A gunshot blotted out the rest of his defiance, and Gus slid to the ground in an inert heap.

Larrupin' Ed shouted: "That man murdered him, Sheriff!"

"He pulled a gun on a deputy!" Ban Shelton rasped back. "Throw down them guns and step back while we take over! Who's that behind the wagon?"

Mike thumbed both guns as he dived for the end of the wagon. No time now to plan further. Gus Delight's foolish outburst had set off a killer's gun and hell had started. Hell that would leave Ban Shelton running the Salt Fork country or stop him here in the scarlet dawn.

Shelton was waiting. His gun blasted as Mike plunged into the open behind the wagon.

The big smoke-blackened coffee pot flew off the tailboard and showered Mike with hot coffee. And as a second shot roared on the heels of the first, Shelton recognized the bandaged head that should have been back in Salt Fork in jail or on the end of a lynch rope.

Shelton yelled and missed the second shot clean. The drive of his spurs sent his horse bolting, with Circle 8 men between him and Mike's guns.

Mike fired over their heads and missed the running horse and crouching figure. The slam of a bullet in his left arm, already wounded, knocked him half around.

That lead came from the gunman that Monte Hill had

pointed out as Montana Jack. The numbing shock left the arm useless as Mike got his other gun up again.

Montana Jack had fired hastily as he reined his horse away. Now he was spurring away after the others.

Mike stumbled past Sam Parks and Jim Crowder and aimed carefully as he emptied the old wooden-handled .45. Montana Jack lurched in the saddle, grabbed the horn, and rode on, wounded but burring tight to the saddle.

Around Mike, guns were crashing, but the targets were moving fast out of range, scattering as they went.

Monte Hill ran past Mike with a rifle and took careful aim. He fired once and missed, coolly levered another cartridge in, and aimed again. His target was the gaunt Parson Pitts, who was riding in a crouch, black coattails flapping in the wind.

Monte Hill's rifle cracked a second time—and a second time he seemed to miss. His angry exclamation was audible as he hastily reloaded.

Then a wild Indian yell came from Guaymas Red. The flapping black coattails were leaving the saddle. Parson Pitts was sliding over, clawing weakly at the saddle horn. Then he seemed to stiffen as he pitched from the saddle.

"Look!" Slim Chance shouted.

The gambler's head and shoulders had hit the damp ground and bounced. And bounced again and again.

The shooting had stopped. Around Mike the men stood frozen as the gambler's foot stayed caught in the stirrup and he was dragged under the driving hoofs of the maddened horse.

Mike thought he heard a thin, far, horrible scream from under the running horse. He wasn't sure. It came no more. The dragging body was limp now, and the coattails had dropped down over the head and were flapping grotesquely as flying hoofs shredded cloth and flesh and bone.

"Shoot the horse!" Mike cried hoarsely.

Monte Hill already had the rifle up. He took his time before squeezing the trigger. And dropped the horse, kicking and helpless, near the top of the slope. The inert body was pinned underneath.

"He come askin' for it," Larrupin' Ed said harshly. "But damned if I wish any man that."

Shelton and the other two men were out of sight now. There'd been no time to look to Gus Delight, who had dragged himself over against the hind wheel of the wagon.

Mike could feel the warm blood over his arm as he stooped by Gus Delight's round, drawn face.

"How bad is it, Gus?"

Gus Delight tried to grin. "Busted up a rib an' missed the lung, I think. I don't feel no blood in my throat. We showed 'em where to get off, didn't we? Ain't that blood on your arm, Mike?"

"Nothing to think about. Get flat on the ground and let's have a look." And Mike called over his shoulder: "Get the horses! There's something funny about that sheriff only bringing three men. I don't. . . ." He broke off, demanding: "What's that?"

Guaymas Red was nearest the back of the wagon, and he, too, had heard the sudden rolling stamp of hoofs, the high, alarmed bellow of startled cattle. Then a fusillade of shots before Guaymas Red could speak.

"Stampede!" Guaymas Red yelled, bolting for his horse.

XII

Under the wagon, Mike caught a glimpse of the cattle coming in a senseless wave of rushing bodies and clashing horns. They'd been started and pointed by a thin line of riders who had come down on them from the east.

Now it was plain why Ban Shelton had come with only three men, why the Circle 8 men had been told to get their time, why

Shelton hadn't stood his ground to fight. Shelton had parlayed while other riders had circled around to get set for surprise and trouble.

The wagon offered some shelter, but the stampede would carry away their horses. They'd be afoot and helpless around the wagon, cold targets for hidden men whose rifles could pick them off one by one.

"Ride it out!" Mike shouted. "Take your guns!"

There was still Gus Delight, helpless on the ground, and for the moment all but forgotten. Mike jumped toward him. Monte Hill got there first, shouting as he lifted Gus Delight's chunky figure.

"Hit the saddle, McBride. I'll do this."

Mike lingered to make sure while the bawling tornado of frightened steers bore down on the spot. The saddled horses that had stayed ground-tied near the wagon through the shooting were catching the panic, too, and starting to move as the Circle 8 men plunged to them.

Monte Hill all but threw Gus Delight into the front of the wagon. Rough treatment, but Gus would have to take it. Mike ran for his horse and it bolted. Then Slim Chance came spurring, stooped far over, caught the dragging reins, and yanked the horse over to Mike.

Larrupin' Ed Shaw had seen how things were with Monte Hill and had gotten his horse and was bringing it at a run.

Mike's arm was still numb to the shoulder. He had to get into the saddle one-handed. He saw blood running over the wrist and fingers as his feet found the stirrups and his good hand took the slack out of the reins. Then the first of the bawling, thundering stampede was on them and the horse needed no spurring as it raced away.

Over his shoulder, Mike saw Monte Hill's horse stumble as a big steer brushed it, and then settle into stride. There was no dust. Ban Shelton's men were plain at the rear of the stampede. Nine or ten of them, at least, shooting forward over the cattle.

They had failed to put the Circle 8 men afoot. Now they were trying to gun them from their horses.

A wild yell over to the right dragged Mike's look. He cursed helplessly as he saw Jim Crowder pitching out of the saddle. Jim's horse kept on. Jim stayed under the torrent of running steers.

Ban Shelton wanted it this way for anyone who stood in the way of his law. Gun law. Shelton law, that could wipe out an old man like Concho Walker and all who tried to stand up to him.

Mike cut over toward Larrupin' Ed and Slim Chance, who were following Guaymas Red and Monte Hill to the west flank of the stampede. Dozy and Sam Parks were coming, also.

They were outnumbered. If they scattered now, they'd stay scattered. The Circle 8 land and cattle would be in other hands.

Looking back, Mike could see the gunmen bunching up to follow them. Ban Shelton and the two men with him evidently hadn't circled fast enough to swing in behind the stampede.

Monte Hill rode close. "Looks like Shelton pulled a trick that'll be hard to beat."

They were plunging over a brushy ridge now, with the stampede swerving off over the lower ground. The Shelton men were following up the slope, shooting as Mike called: "Ain't a chance to whip that bunch! Scatter the boys an' keep riding! Shelton's men'll give up after a few miles!"

Monte Hill nodded. His look was regretful, disappointed. Mike McBride was quitting after all his talk of blocking Shelton.

They topped the ridge and raced down through the brush, hidden for a little from the guns behind. Mike lagged, swinging to the left. Monte Hill caught up with Larrupin' Ed and the others, urging them ahead.

Dozy and Sam Parks passed on as Mike pulled his horse hard over along the ridge, paralleling the top. Brush and low trees closed in behind him. When he'd ridden a hundred and fifty yards and pulled up, the others were out of sight, crashing on down the slope.

Mike dismounted behind low bushes as the Shelton men topped the ridge in a bunch, quirting, spurring after the fleeing riders ahead. They swept on down the slope without looking toward the brush where Mike waited.

Blood covered Mike's left hand, and the throbbing hurt went up into the shoulder. But he could use the hand a little and reload both six-guns. His rifle was back in Salt Fork.

He was in the saddle again when he heard another coming. The man cut the ridge and took the slope. His hat was black; he showed in the clear for an instant, and he was the gunman deputy that Monte Hill had called Lafe Cantwell.

Ragged bursts of gunfire marked the running fight moving off into the west. No one followed Cantwell as Mike put his horse into a run south along the ridge.

Minutes later the distant gunfire in the west seemed to double in intensity, as if the Circle 8 men had been caught and had turned to fight. Mike fought down the urge to head that way fast. His grim face was lined with strain as he kept on.

The grub wagon was out there on the sun-drenched flat. Parson Pitts horse was dead and had been rolled off the body. Two saddled horses stood restlessly nearby, and the two men near the body were talking with some heat.

Dude Ringold, handsome, well-dressed, had a neck sling supporting his left arm. His voice was angrily clear as Mike stepped behind a small tree and listened.

"You're talkin' a lot, but it don't change me, Shelton. I shot that damn' lamp out last night and put the lead in the old coot's back and got a bullet in my arm for it. I've earned Parson's share, and I want it for the time I'll be laid up from gambling."

"The idea was mine and Parson's in the first place," Shelton rasped. "There ain't too much to go around as it is, with that lawyer cuttin' in for his share."

"You can't claim the Circle Eight, Shelton. There'll be enough talk as it is. That greasy little lawyer ain't to be trusted, an' Brazos hasn't got the head or tongue for this. You've got to have me to handle the Circle Eight. I'll have my price for it or nobody cashes in. Savvy?"

"Brazos don't think fast, but he'll do what he's told," Ban Shelton sneered. "Dude, you've growed a big head for a young fellow."

Dude Ringold jumped back, grabbing under his coat. Then the vomiting six-gun in Ban Shelton's hand slammed him against the earth and he stayed there, trying weakly to get his gun out.

Ban Shelton tore the gun from him, threw it away, and grinned down at the dying man.

"That's your cut, Dude. Parson an' me was savin' it for you." Shelton was not a hundred yards away, back partly turned to the crest of the slope as Mike stepped out toward him.

"I'll take your money belt. You won't need it," Shelton said as he knelt by the young gambler. He had jerked the money belt out and was getting to his feet when Mike spoke.

"I've brought your cut, Shelton."

Ban Shelton whirled around—and for an instant his angular face was stunned, unbelieving. Then he hurled the belt aside and his pearl handled gun streaked from the holster, blasting as it came out.

Mike's gun met shot for shot, handicapped by the sun into which he was facing. A bullet nicked his ear. Shelton staggered as lead tore into his leg. His gun emptied as he reached for Dude Ringold's gun, and he made a lurching dive and caught up the gambler's gun.

One-handed, Mike dropped his empty gun and caught the other from under his belt without stopping his advance.

That broke Ban Shelton's nerve. He made a limping break for his horse, which jumped back nervously.

Mike ran forward. He had three shots left and no time to reload if Shelton started riding. Shelton got the reins and cursed the horse wildly as he caught the saddle and swung awkwardly up.

For an instant he was silhouetted against the blazing morning sun. Mike stopped, steadied, and emptied the second gun in a roaring roll of shots that hurled Ban Shelton out of the saddle in a sprawling fall as the horse bolted away.

Mike stood grimly by the man as he died. He had had the feeling, when he sighted Shelton a few minutes back, that it would end this way.

Shelton died first, with Dude Ringold lying on his side, staring at the sight with a thin, fixed grin.

Mike looked around. His voice was husky. "Concho, I didn't aim to make the start this way. You figure it out."

He went back for his horse and rode to the wagon. Gus Delight was still alive. He'd keep on living.

Gus was on the ground again, with his shirt off, when the first of a straggling line of riders swept down on them.

Larrupin' Ed and Monte Hill were leading. Close behind them galloped the buckskin-clad figure of old Jubal Lark.

"Don't know what happened, but it looks good," Mike said to Gus Delight.

The riders were around them a few moments later. Strange faces riding up. Smiling faces that gathered around while Jubal Lark leaped down, brandishing an old rifle and whooping.

"How's this fer fixin' your business, boy? I cotched that snaky little law talker in his office as he was a-fixin' to ride to Shelton's ranch. Sawed a knife ag'in' his throat an' he talked an' give me the papers Concho signed an' left with him. He squealed as how them gamblers an' a sheriff's posse was comin' to get your cattle at daybreak, all legal an' nice."

Jubal spat again and continued: "I taken him to the young doc to tell his story. Shelton's sister was there, a-talkin' already. They studied the papers Concho signed an' heered the lawyer talk again, an' the doc run out to see men he said'd like to know all this. Took some time to get 'em all together an' stop at a ranch er two fer more men afore we come a-ridin' hard to meet the sheriff at his dirty work. An' we met a runnin' gunfight an' heered the news. How bad you hurt, boy?"

"Not bad," Mike said. "The sheriff's dead. He killed Dude Ringold and shot it out with me."

"When I got a good look back and saw that Shelton wasn't with his men," Monte Hill said, "I had an idea maybe you still had him on your mind, after all. We headed this way as quick as possible." And he said slowly: "So Ban's dead at last."

"Come help haze them steers back, mister," Jubal Lark urged Monte Hill. "An' then we'll git to Salt Fork an' celebrate."

"Wasn't there some business you had to see about quick in Salt Fork this morning?" Mike said to Monte Hill. "Some Texas business you never finished?"

"I'll help here first, McBride."

"Steers can wait, and my business is mostly settled," Mike said, grinning faintly. "Not knowing about such things, I'd say your business has waited long enough. I'm obliged for everything . . . and good luck in Salt Fork."

★ ★ ★ ★ ★

KILLER COME HOME

★ ★ ★ ★ ★

This was also a short novel that Ted Flynn knew beforehand would be sold to Jack Burr at Street and Smith's *Western Story*. It was completed on September 20, 1939, ran sixty-eight typescript pages, and was without a title. The author was paid $400.00 for this, the eighth story he wrote in 1939. Upon publication it was showcased all by itself on the cover of *Western Story* (1/20/40) as "Killer Come Home! A book-length novel by T.T. Flynn."

I

The Reno Kid had been riding across that harsh sun-baked country for hours, and every time he looked back the yellow dust cloud hung in the distance.

This had been bunch-grass land, with scattered sagebrush and prickly pear. Never too good, it was worthless now under the searing blight of drought. Overhead not a cloud marred the blue sky. The afternoon sun was a copper blaze. Heat shimmered above the baked soil. The wind was a breath from an open furnace, and, when it blew, dust swirled and spiraling dust devils wandered across the landscape.

The Reno Kid's horse was crusted with white, dried sweat. Dust layers were yellowish-white against the black hide. Two hours back the horse had stopped sweating. The Reno Kid was drying out fast, too, and the reason was the untouched canteen that hung from the saddle horn.

There had been two canteens. A bullet had punctured the largest. There had been a pack horse; a bullet had left it stretched back there at the Stinking Rocks, which was Strickland King's outer water hole to the west.

Two King gunmen had been guarding that fenced-in skim of water and circle of cracked mud. The man who had recognized the Reno Kid and opened fire wouldn't be doing any more shooting for a while. The other had dived for his horse and fled through the hot, dry morning.

The Reno Kid's pack horse had been shot down, two bullet

holes put through his hat, his best canteen punctured. But when the shooting was over, he was free to cut the wire and lead his saddle horse across the cracking mud to water.

The big sign at the Stinking Rocks had said: *KEEP OUTSIDE THIS WIRE.* Unwittingly the Reno Kid had ridden out of the north into a drought-parched land and a water war.

Strickland King's country—Strickland King's water—Strickland King's gunmen. Maybe the King gunman who had recognized him had thought him still too young to be much of a threat. Maybe the reward had made the man reckless. Guns had been crashing before the two King men realized they were fighting for their lives.

Now when the Reno Kid looked back, the faint yellow dust cloud was there behind him. His cracked lips hurt a little as he smiled grimly. He hadn't thought other King riders would be so near. They'd been after him in less than an hour. He'd had to start pushing his horse.

The canteen of water might have kept him and the horse going through the night and into the next day if they could have taken things easy. But the horse would be finished by night now if he didn't get water and rest. And it was all of a hundred miles from the Stinking Rocks to the next water hole—unless there was water at a place called Murphy's Well. The Reno Kid had heard about Murphy's Well but had never been past the spot.

"A short day's ride southwest of the Stinkin' Rocks," an old border rat had told him years back. "Most folks don't know about it, but if you ever get dry over in there, son, don't fergit it. You lay a line from the Stinkin' Rocks past Horn Butte, which brings you off the trail an' down acrost Dry Bone Flat. An' right where you'd never expect to find any water, there's three big jaggedy rocks a couple hundred feet high with a old dug well between 'em."

When the Reno Kid wanted to know more about it, the

prospector had explained.

"I knowed Pat Murphy who found water there back in the late 'Sixties. Pat was a water witch an' witched hisself water sign there. He dug down an' derned if he didn't strike wet. The Apaches got Pat that same year over on the Gila. But the sojers had heard about the water find, and, after they rounded the Injuns up, they sent men over to Pat's rocks an' timbered 'em in a well, jest to have water handy around that dry stretch. Ain't been used hardly since, but I was past there last year an' the timbers was still good an' there was water at the bottom. Jest remember it, son. They's times when you find wet water mighty handy."

Horn Butte was behind, off in the northeast now, thrusting its rocky horn toward the brassy sky. There was a slight haze low down, far off against the northern horizon. That would be the high crests of the mountains where timber was parched and fire-dry, and springs and streams were trickles at best and dry for the most part.

The Reno Kid swore softly through his parched lips. The land was breaking into raw gullies and ridges, and far beyond the breaks lay a vast flat reaching thirty miles and more to low hills, just as dry and barren as the rest of the country.

Here and there on that flat were great, fantastically shaped rocks. In the shimmering, hazy distance, dwarfed by the miles of space, three saw-toothed rocks jutted toward the sky.

The Reno Kid narrowed his dust-rimmed eyes and stared at the rocks a long time as he rode forward. And finally he shook his head.

"It's them, but if there's water there now, I'm a lizard."

Stiffly the Reno Kid turned in the saddle and looked back. For a few moments the sweep of space back there seemed clear—and then the faint telltale haze drifted up into visibility.

Blood in their eyes and hell in their hearts. They're gonna get me or know why. Strickland King must be paying plenty to keep 'em on a dry trail like this. The Reno Kid grinned faintly. *Ain't any easier on them than it is on me. Maybe the end'll be harder if we get to that water witch's hole.*

He dismounted, untied the canteen, and dribbled some of the warm water into his mouth. He had to elbow the horse's head aside as he stood with his head back, washing the water around in his dry mouth and letting it trickle, drop by drop, down his throat.

He lifted the canteen for another swallow, then stared at the dried froth on the horse's jaw.

"That swallow sure was sweet. But you've got work to do, horse. Here goes . . . and I hope I'm right."

The crown of his hat was punctured. Not enough water to do much good in the hat, anyway. The Reno Kid shrugged. He forced the horse's head up, shoved the canteen back in the jaws, and let the horse have moisture by trickles. Half the water was wasted and the animal was trembling for more when the last drop was gone.

"Now we'll see," said the Reno Kid huskily as he hooked the empty canteen back over the saddle horn and mounted.

The dust cloud had moved nearer. But those riders back there weren't killing their horses. They seemed to know that, if they followed grimly, steadily, they'd run the man and horse ahead of them out of water.

The Reno Kid fumbled back in a saddle pocket, brought out a fresh box of cartridges, and filled the empty loops in his belt. The saddle pockets bulged with cartridges for his handgun and the Winchester in the leather saddle boot.

He made a lonely speck against the parched vastness of Dry Bone Flat as he rode on. The sun was growing in size as it slid down toward the jagged line of hills that formed the western horizon. Stunted tarbush plants cast thin twisted shadows toward the east, and, when the Reno Kid turned his head, the big, fantastic shadow he and the horse made seemed to be stalking their heels.

"Hell of a place to end up in," he muttered.

The water hadn't done him much good. His mouth felt too small for his tongue. The horse, too, was almost done. When the sun had slid far down toward those western hills, the Reno Kid halted on a slight rise of ground and studied the back trail.

Miles back, tiny black dots crawled relentlessly across the baked earth after him. But the three saw-toothed rocks were not far ahead now. They grew rapidly in size as the Reno Kid rode toward them.

The sun had vanished in a final blaze of light; the quick coolness of twilight was shutting down when the Reno Kid reached the saw-tooth rocks. Red and sheer they towered two hundred feet and more from the dry plain. Weathered rubble formed little mounds around the outside base.

Seen close, the rocks proved to be one mass that formed the sides of a triangle, boxing in a crooked V-shaped, sandy enclosure some twenty yards across and opening to the south. His horse bolted the last few hundred yards and followed wagon tracks and hoof marks into the V-opening, and came to halt, blowing and trembling.

Back in the V was the well opening. The Reno Kid had known it would be there when he saw the wagon tracks. He stopped the horse's rush to the well curb and swung down. As eager as the horse, he stumbled in his effort to reach the gnarled cedar trunks that formed the well curb.

The Reno Kid bent over the edge. Down in the damp cool shadows that filled the timbered shaft the motionless sheen of water lay thirty feet and more below.

The shaft timbers had not rotted. The old windlass was still there, still serviceable, with rotted strands of rope around the drum. But there was no rope, no bucket.

The Reno Kid grinned, shook out his well-stretched saddle rope. Hurriedly he dumped the boxed cartridges out of the saddlebags and tied the rope to the leather strip that connected the bags. The deep leather pockets would hold water in plenty.

The Reno Kid had to elbow the snorting horse aside as he lowered the bags into the well.

"Coming quick, old-timer," he promised huskily.

He could see marks on the well timbers where the water level usually stayed much nearer the surface. But it didn't matter, as long as there was water in the bottom.

The saddle rope he carried was short. Only a foot or two was left in his hand when the leather bags splashed hollowly below, and lost air with sudden gurgles as they went under.

The Reno Kid was weak, feverish with the terrible water hunger that gnawed at every parched pore. He was leaning over the well curb with the last of the short rope paid out when the bags sank from sight. He sloshed the bags up and down to let the last of the air gurgle out of the pockets.

And when he pulled up, the bags came into sight, glistening, heavy with the water filling the pockets. The sound of the drops cascading off was like music.

The black horse, half maddened by thirst, thrust close, nosing down toward the sound of falling water. His shoulder pushed the Reno Kid off balance, set his feet slipping in the sand. The man swore, grabbed frantically to keep from falling down into the well. The taut rope slipped in his fingers and was gone before he realized what was happening.

The saddlebags chunked heavily back into the water. The rope snaked down on top of them and sank from sight.

The water was already smoothing back into a mocking, glassy surface as the Reno Kid pushed himself upright and began to curse in a dry, terrible monotone.

"I oughta throw you down after it!" he cried furiously to the horse. "You fixed us now!"

He caught the reins and pulled the animal back lest it stagger into the well in its frantic eagerness to get at the water.

Then he stood for a moment, forcing himself to be calm. He rolled a cigarette with unsteady fingers, lighted it, put it in his mouth. But he threw it aside with a grimace as the hot acrid smoke burned against his swollen tongue.

He looked down in the well again. The small cedar tree trunks that formed the sides might give a man footing to climb down to the water. But if the man was too weak to get back up, or something about the well siding gave way, he'd stay down there at the bottom—cold meat for any gunmen hanging around to get him.

Clothes might be cut into strips to make a weak line that would lower the small canteen down and bring it up. But that would take time.

The Reno Kid hauled himself heavily into the saddle and spurred the unwilling horse away from the well, out of the enclosed V to where he could look through the twilight to the back trail.

The pursuit was in view now, out there across the flat—four of them as near as he could judge.

II

Calculating the distance his pursuers had to travel, the Reno Kid knew there wasn't time to get that small canteen down to water. Not now, and probably not through the night. He'd never have a chance while those bunched riders were anywhere close.

Sand had drifted over the bones of two dead burros at his left. Other bones were in sight. The broken frame of an old wagon had been abandoned at one side of the V-opening. Outside and inside the V you could see sign where men had camped, thrown away their gear, where animals had died. And if the Reno Kid wasn't mistaken, off there a couple of hundred yards were low mounds with wooden headboards that marked graves.

You could see where the dry years of the past had brought men and animals face to face with death and thirst here at Murphy's Well. And as the last shadows of the day stretched, dark and purple across the dry earth, death seemed to crawl in with the coming night.

The Reno Kid rode around the saw-toothed rocks, taking stock of his position. And what he saw plastered a grim smile on his face as he rode back to the opening.

He rode inside, dismounted, and tied the horse to a pinnacle of rock back in the V. Here and there split-off pieces of rock lay half buried in the sand, and more were outside.

The Reno Kid began to carry rocks to the opening, working fast. He was staggering with exhaustion by the time he had a small breastwork three feet across and less than two feet high. He ran to the old wagon, wrenched off a seat board, used it as a shovel to scoop a small trench in the sand behind the rocks.

The horsemen were not half a mile away when the Reno Kid threw the board aside and lurched, sobbing for breath, to the horse. He caught his rifle from the saddle boot, dumped boxes of cartridges into the trench, and collapsed on the rocks, panting, trembling with weakness.

Four riders. The light had faded until they were only dark blurs out there on the plain. They were scattering out now, rifles ready. Steady again, the Reno Kid put a shot over their heads.

They stopped. The Reno Kid could hear them calling to one another. One figure rode cautiously forward.

"We're gonna take you back, feller! Dead or alive! Which'll it be?"

"Got a sheriff or a deputy or a warrant along?"

"We got all we need!"

The Reno Kid answered through his cupped hands. "Ride back an' tell Strickland King I've staked out this water hole. I got food, plenty of water, an' enough cartridges to hold out a week. You'll be dried to jerky meat before you gun me out of here. Ride back while you can make it an' I'll move on across the border."

He fired another shot high, and the man yelled something and galloped back to his companions. They talked a little and turned on the back trail. They were heading back toward the Stinking Rocks when night swallowed them.

The Reno Kid grinned coldly. They'd be back under cover of darkness, Indian style, rushing the low makeshift barricade fronting the shallow trench. Reward money was easy money, and they had not ridden all day and cornered their man to turn back so meekly now.

Maybe they'd get him, too. Four guns against one had a good chance.

But if they didn't, if he could hold them off until daybreak and no other King men arrived, they were whipped. They couldn't have brought much water along. They'd have to turn back fast to the Stinking Rocks water.

Daybreak was a long time away, though—a lifetime away to a man who was dried out to the bones. The Reno Kid's tongue was larger. Thought of the cool, clear water so near was maddening. And he couldn't make a try at it until he knew the pursuit was turned back.

No moon tonight. Stars were popping out against the sable sky, but the stars didn't do much to the dark murky mass of night close to the ground.

Hours passed. The Reno Kid's ears hurt with the strain of listening. Once he heard the mocking babble of coyotes, whispering through space. Coyotes had to live, even when it meant hunting meat on the baked hopeless expanse of Dry Bone Flat.

"I ain't as good as a damned coyote," he growled. "They can hunt and hooraw while I've got to sit here by that damned water and wait. God, for one big swallow of it . . . shut up, damn you!"

The Reno Kid had caught himself talking aloud. Dreaming. He began to think of a white-water stream in the Jackson Hole country where he'd once camped. Shade and green grass. Fresh fish broiling over the fire. Cool water to drink and splash around in during the heat of the day.

"Ain't you got any sense?" the Reno Kid croaked to himself. "You'll he hollering an' singing and running out there, scooping water oft the sand. And them damned gun-toters of King's'll ride up behind and blast you right over into that deep Jordan River that parsons preach about."

The sounds out there in the night were incessant. None of them meant anything. Time after time the Reno Kid came to a tense crouch, gun ready, at some slight night sound or movement out there in the dark. And each time he was mistaken.

But those damned bounty hunters were out there. They were out there somewhere, closing in on foot. No use to think they'd ridden through the long scorching day to let a few words turn them back. Not four to one, with night to help them.

Waiting, nerves on edge, finger crooked by the rifle trigger, was worse than a roaring gunfight. Better be dead or free to get at that cool water down the well shaft. Just one swallow. . . .

The Reno Kid muttered another curse at himself for thinking of the water, and began to pad back and forth on the sand. Maybe the King men were near enough to hear his steps. Maybe this would draw their fire. Get it over with.

Suddenly the Reno Kid stopped short, peering into the night. Smoothly he brought the Winchester up, finger crooked on the trigger. Somebody was moving out there. Feet were whispering across the sand.

He had a moment of doubt. The sound was too plain. Ears must be tricking him again. But the sounds continued. Soft steps were coming from the right. Probably there were more out to the left, also, as the other three King men closed in.

The Reno Kid loosened the six-gun in his holster, crept to the low rock barricade, and poised for the first visible movement.

He did not have to wait. A fragment of the night moved out there where the feet whispered on the sand. If he waited a moment, it would be a sure shot. If he fired now, he'd spook the rest of their guns out and know where they were. The Reno Kid sighted on the uncertain target and squeezed the trigger.

The shot crashed into the night. A scream cut through the desert quiet. The Reno Kid leaped back of the low barricade and pumped another shell ready.

Then as his mind separated that scream from the sound of the shot, he froze, staring into the blackness. That had been a woman's scream.

No guns had answered his shot. No other sound was out there in the night. The Reno Kid croaked: "Who's there?"

There was no reply. He felt sick. Must have killed a woman. *Killed a woman.* He couldn't wait and think about it. He had to go out there and see.

Weak from the dread of what he was going to find, the Reno Kid made a crouching run to the spot, knowing that if the King men were out there, they'd gun him down for sure.

Then he heard her moan. A moment later he was beside her. His groping hand touched soft hair. A small shoulder moved convulsively under his fingers.

His foot caught in a coil of rope and there was a metallic rattle as he kicked the foot free. Sounded like a metal bucket.

Then the woman was moaning: "No. No." She fought off his hand and tried to sit up.

"I didn't know you were a woman!" the Reno Kid gulped. "Where'd it hit you? I . . . I'll make a light an' see what I can do."

"Who are you?" she gasped.

"It doesn't matter," said the Reno Kid. "I'd rather have been hung than do a thing like this. Lady, where'd it hit you?"

She stood up, made little movements in the dark. "You must have missed me," she said in a shaking voice. "It frightened me so bad that I . . . I fainted."

"Oh, thank God!" the Reno Kid exploded in relief. And then, man-like, he was irritated. "What'd you want to sneak up like this in the middle of the night and almost make me kill you? Away out here from nowhere where a woman ain't got any call to be in the first place."

Her voice, when she answered him, was cold: "This is free government land. What right did you have to shoot at me? Has Strickland King dared to close up this water, too?"

"I ain't a King man," the Reno Kid told her. "I'm camping here waiting for King's gunnies to come shooting. I thought you were one of them. What's this rope on the ground?"

"It's a rope and a bucket. I walked on ahead of the wagon to draw some fresh water."

"I thought it was. Let me draw some water," the Reno kid said thickly. "I ain't had any way to draw water out of that well."

He was already groping on the ground for the rope. He broke into a stumbling run toward the well, heedless of any King men who might be closing in through the dark.

This time the rope did not slip. The bucket came up dripping and half full. The Reno Kid slopped water over his face, chin, shirt, and vest as he tried to hold that terrible water hunger down to sparing sips.

He was panting when he forced himself to put the bucket at his feet and wait a little.

The girl spoke at his elbow. "You . . . you said the King men were trying to shoot you?"

"Seen any of 'em out there anywhere?"

"No."

"Four of 'em trailed me all day. I had a little gun trouble with 'em at the Stinking Rocks."

She misunderstood. "Strickland King's keeping his water," she said bitterly. "Not a drop for dying sheep, cattle, and horses. No water even for women and children. The only water Strickland King is giving away these days is a barrelful to men who'll give up their homesteads and drive out of South Valley for good."

"Nesters in South Valley, huh?" the Reno Kid muttered.

"So you're a cowman, too," she flared back at him. "I can tell by the way you talk. You're one of the kind who like to see desperate, hardworking people lose everything. You make families go hungry and children cry for water while hired gunmen keep them thirsty. If the King men are hunting you, it's one wolf breed after another of the same kind."

The Reno Kid lifted the bucket and drank again. He was smiling grimly in the darkness.

"Spunky, ain't you, ma'am? But don't blame me for King's tricks. I never made any woman go hungry or kept water from kids. I'm going to water my horse out of this bucket."

She seemed to have no objection, but her voice was still bitter. "I wouldn't keep water from any living thing. I know what it means to be thirsty. First let me drink. I've walked a long way ahead of the wagon without water."

"Here," said the Reno Kid hastily, and, as she took the wet bucket, he groped for a match. When he heard her put the bucket down, he snapped the match into flame and held it up so he could see what manner of woman he had shot at.

The Reno Kid swallowed as her dark eyes looked into the match flame and her hand pushed back hair black as the night around them.

He had guessed her to be not too old. Now he saw that she was as young as himself. Clearly she was tired, and her face had traces of work, worry, and scanty food. But she was standing straight, fearless, with a sort of wild, proud defiance. Maybe she wasn't exactly pretty, but, as the match burned down and out, the Reno Kid thought she was the loveliest girl he had ever seen. Something about the proud independence of her caught at him.

"Some folks call me Slim," he said gruffly. "What's your name?"

"Nancy Willis," she answered. "And if you're afraid that King's men are going to shoot you, a light won't help you, will it?"

The Reno Kid laughed softly.

"It helped me see the prettiest girl I've ever run across, ma'am. That's worth plenty of risk."

"Not to me," said Nancy Willis coolly.

The Reno Kid was lowering the bucket into the well again. "You got a wagon coming out there, ma'am?"

"Yes."

"Did King give you folks a barrel of water to leave on?"

"He'd like to," Nancy Willis said scornfully. "He'd like to burn us out and shoot us out. He'd like to dry us out and starve us out. But there are some things even Strickland King doesn't dare do. Old Tobe Barrett, the sheriff, isn't afraid of King, and there are others who will back Tobe up if he's trying to carry out the law. Strickland King tries to make everything legal."

The Reno Kid couldn't see her face, but he knew it must be reflecting the sorrow in her voice.

"Last year his gunmen killed my father . . . and they made it look like the right was on their side. They'd like an excuse to kill Bud, my younger brother. I won't even let Bud carry a gun any more. He wouldn't have a chance if they caught him out alone and started a quarrel. We're going to stay on our land and outlast Strickland King. Someday the rains will come again, and, when they do, we'll be waiting on our own land."

"Sounds like you will," the Reno Kid agreed. "But you're hauling water a long way, ma'am."

"Almost forty miles," said Nancy Willis. "South Creek is dry. The spring that feeds the east fork is still flowing, but it's on Strickland King's land and he's dammed the water back and fenced everyone out."

"Since when did Strickland King own land around that spring, ma'am?" the Reno Kid asked quickly.

"He doesn't," said Nancy Willis. "But he leases it from a lawyer named Jackson in Canfield. Oh, it's legal enough. We've tried everything. There's nothing we can do but look at the dry sand in South Creek and wait for rain."

The bucket came up, dripping full. The Reno Kid rested it on the well curb for a minute and muttered: "Forty miles out and forty miles back. How long does a load of water last?"

"Not long," Nancy said. "Our wagon doesn't do much else but haul water these days. We have about the only animals left in the valley that can stand the trip. We give some of the water away, and trade some of it for feed to keep the oxen going."

Silently the Reno Kid carried the water over to his horse, and went back for more. "Where's your wagon?" he asked.

"Coming," she said. "We used our last water before dark. I rode all afternoon and felt like walking ahead. Bud and Jerry and Mister Meeks stayed with the wagon."

"Who's Meeks?"

"Our nearest neighbor. I've been trying to keep him and his

family from moving away by giving them water." Her voice took on that fierce, stubborn note again. "It will rain. If I can keep Strickland King from driving people out, they'll have water one of these days and be strong again."

The Reno Kid carried the second bucket to his horse, and under his breath muttered again: "Forty miles out an' forty back for water. An' then giving the water away to make 'em wait out King." When he turned back to the well, he said: "I was going to hold this well for myself. But I reckon your wagon can come in and fill up. If there's trouble, tell your brothers to keep back and out of it."

"This is free water," Nancy said coldly. "If you and King's men want to kill each other off, it's no concern of ours."

The Reno Kid chuckled. "I'll take a heap of killing after that cold drink. Better stay back in here while I keep watch. It's a wonder those skunks haven't jumped us by now. They're up to something and taking their time about it."

Beyond the low rock barricade the night was still empty of sound. Watching intently, rifle ready, the Reno Kid thought of Nancy Willis and the nester trouble.

It was the old story. The crop men came in like the plague, put up their fences, multiplied like grasshoppers, and were twice as destructive. For grasshoppers moved on and the land came back. Nesters dug in and the range was ruined for good. And these people who grubbed and worked in the dirt hung on like grim death. Look at this wagon coming for water. Sensible settlers would have given up long ago and moved on.

After a little the Reno Kid heard the wagon coming in. A bullwhip cracked like a pistol shot. A voice urged the oxen. Axles creaked. And then someone shouted: "Oh-h, Nancy! Nancy!"

"Here, Bud!" the girl called back. She had moved up close to the Reno Kid.

"Are you all right, Nancy?" the voice demanded.

"Yes."

The wagon came on. Bud's voice spoke anxiously. "We thought we heard a shot."

The Reno Kid answered.

"You did. But the lady's all right. Drive in here an' get your water. And keep away from me. I'm watching for a bunch of buzzards that are around somewhere."

Bud made no reply to that. The lumbering wagon loomed up out of the night with the wagon sheet looking like a small ghostly cloud.

"I've got some rocks piled up here," the Reno Kid warned. "Swing your teams around them."

"Where?" a husky voice answered, and two figures strode forward.

The Reno Kid bit off his answer as he caught the soft jingle of spur chains. Nesters driving oxen didn't wear spurs.

"Keep still," the Reno Kid rapped as a crouching jump carried him to one side.

III

A gun roared a flaming answer. A second gun joined in as the Reno Kid fired the rifle and dodged again, palming his side gun.

Two men and a third appeared at the heads of the lead oxen and opened fire. A bullet burned the Reno Kid's left arm as one of the dark figures collapsed. The streaking flame of his handgun flipped at the muzzle flashes marking the next man.

And suddenly there was only one gun left, firing fast, wildly, as the six-shooter in the Reno Kid's hand clicked empty. He shoved the empty gun under his belt and cocked the Winchester as he sprawled to the ground. With no light to aim by, he threw the rifle sights instinctively like a pistol, waited for a muzzle

125

flash before firing. And then his man was floundering and gasping on the ground.

The Reno Kid backed away from the spot, reloading the handgun. An ox was threshing on the ground, the other oxen plunging, floundering in fright. And in shot-echoing ears the Reno Kid heard a voice warning: "Keep down, Nancy! Stay here!"

"You're hurt, Bud!" Nancy Willis cried out. "Oh, you're shot!"

Out in the night horses came running and a man shouted: "Get him all right, boys?"

The Reno Kid walked out with the rifle ready. The horses boiled up to the wagon and the man leaped from the saddle with the reins of the other men's mounts.

"That was the trick to get him quick an' safe!" he burst out jubilantly. "Two thousand reward to divvy up fer no work a-tall!"

"Slick trick," answered the Reno Kid. "Here's a slicker one. Reach high."

A muffled oath came as the man froze before the rifle muzzle. His lifting hands carried up the reins of three led horses.

"Three to one ought to have done it," the Reno Kid told him. "But it didn't. Want a chance for your gun and a try at getting all that reward money for yourself?"

The man sullenly refused. "I know when I ain't got a chance. Them damn' farmers must've helped you get the boys. Strickland King'll have something to say about that."

"Has Strickland King been elected sheriff?" the Reno Kid inquired.

"Hell, no."

"Then it ain't his business and you coyotes on his payroll yapped your way after the wrong deer. Turn around." He took the man's gun belt and called: "Break a light out of the wagon there!"

A match flared under the wagon sheet, a lantern glowed out,

swung to the ground, and bobbed toward them.

The light showed two bodies motionless on the sand and a third man holding his middle and groaning. The floundering ox lay with neck twisted in the heavy wooden yoke and blood coming from its mouth.

A lanky, raw-boned man with a stubble of beard stood staring at the oxen. "Thet Baldy ox's got blood on his laig," he said tremulously. "He won't be no good, neither."

"And you damn' dirt scratchers won't be no good when Strickland King hears how you helped this damn' outlaw kill his men," the prisoner snarled.

"King can't blame us fer this," the lanky man protested apprehensively. "You men took over the wagon back there an' said you was huntin' an outlaw. We didn't have no part in it."

"If I'd had me a gun, I'd've poured lead into 'em so fast they'd 'a' splattered!" the lantern holder shrilled furiously. "Wasn't no call for you damn' King gun-toters to use us fer a blind while you throwed lead all around my sister!"

He was short, scrawny, and ragged, with hot anger on his face. Not more than twelve or thirteen, the Reno Kid guessed, and looking a lot like his sister.

Nancy Willis came forward and snatched the lantern. "That's enough, Jerry," she said sternly. "Another word and I'll send you in the wagon."

Jerry faced his sister hotly, fists clenched.

"Ain't menfolks got a right to talk up when maybe their sister's been hurt? I've took all I aim to take from this damn' King bunch. Treatin' us like dogs an' runnin' over us every chance they get. An now fannin' their damn' guns like it didn't matter whether you was kilt or not. I tell you. . . ."

"Jerry! Get in that wagon! Isn't it bad enough without your swearing disgracefully and making more trouble?"

The youngster choked on helpless fury as he darted to the

wagon and scrambled inside.

"Spunky," said the Reno Kid with a faint smile.

"The little pup'll button his mouth when King evens up fer this," the prisoner growled.

"King ain't here now," the Reno Kid said. "Next word out of you will rile me."

The prisoner glared from a thin hard face roughened by a week's growth of black beard. He was the man who had fled from the Stinking Rocks.

"If he worries you again, ma'am," the Reno Kid spoke to Nancy Willis, "I'll gag him or part his hair with a gun barrel."

The lantern light showed her pale face strained and bitter.

"What do I care how any killer feels?" she choked. "I'm thinking about what you've done to us."

"Me, ma'am?"

"You!" Nancy blazed. "If you hadn't been here with blood on your hands and outlaw money on your head, this wouldn't have happened. Look at us. One of our oxen dead and another crippled. And Bud over there with his knee torn by a bullet so he can't walk."

"I'm sorry, ma'am."

"Do you know how to be sorry for anything?" she demanded. "How will we get the wagon back, much less take home any water? You've killed men and wounded others, but you'll ride on with your neck safe. And we'll get back some way without any hope left. And then you egg Jerry on and threaten this man, so there won't be any doubt that Strickland King will find a way to blame us for all this. He's been waiting for such a chance. Every homesteading family left in South Valley will pay for this."

"You bet they will," the prisoner snapped.

The Reno Kid was grinning as he turned on the man, and in the lantern light his face made the man step back involuntarily and lift a shielding arm.

The nearest horse moved uneasily as the Reno Kid stepped to him, watching the prisoner. The Reno Kid shook out the coiled saddle rope, flipped a small loop over the prisoner's head, and yanked it tight.

"For that," he said, "you get hog-tied like a dirty horse thief. Which maybe wouldn't be far wrong, at that. Git down on the ground."

"You're making it harder for us," Nancy protested hotly.

Silently the Reno Kid tied the prisoner's elbows and legs behind the back, so that the noose stayed taut on the man's neck.

"Stroking a rattler's back never milked the poison out of his fangs, ma'am. Tell your brother Jerry to hold these horses, and look to your other brother while I help this long-legged plow-man."

"We don't want any help."

"You're getting it," said the Reno Kid unsmilingly. "Let me have that lantern." He took it from her hand. Jerry was already scrambling out of the wagon.

"Gosh, m-mister," the youngster stuttered as he grabbed the reins. "You sure showed 'em how to shoot. Someday I'll be like that."

"Not if your sister can help it."

"Shucks, women don't understand," Jerry said scornfully. "Didja kill them skunks clean?"

The Reno Kid examined the two bodies. Hard-looking men, one bearded, one with only a reddish stubble. The Kid had seen a thousand like them along the border, east on the Texas cattle trails, and skulking around Indian Territory. Any man could buy them if the pay was right.

The third man was the same type, older, with a black mustache. He was shot through the side and hip, and groaning and holding his side.

"I cain't move, hardly. I got to have water."

"You'll get it," said the Reno Kid. "Move that hand away so I can see this hole in your side. Bleeding some, but I've seen worse. Here's where it comes out in back with some rib. Clean-looking blood. No air bubbles. Stop that bellowing and crawling and we'll tie you up."

When he had done so, the Reno Kid added the wounded man's gun belt to the others he had collected.

"Your name Meeks?" he said to the lanky, apprehensive nester.

"Uhn-huh."

"Stop sweating about what'll happen to you someday and get that ox out of the yoke and the wagon up to the well. Start a fire and heat up some water and then fix grub."

"We ain't got a chance now," Meeks complained.

"A rabbit like you never had a chance," the Reno Kid said impatiently. "Here, button. Hold the lantern for him."

Beyond the oxen Nancy Willis was kneeling by a sitting figure. When the Reno Kid stepped there and struck a match, he saw a slim young man of about eighteen who had slit his overalls up above the right knee and had torn his shirt into strips that he was tying on a bloody knee.

A second match showed blood oozing rather than spurting from the knee.

"Have you fixed up in no time," the Reno Kid decided. "Too bad you got messed up like this in my private feuding."

Bud Willis shrugged as the match went out. His voice was calm.

"King would have tripped us up one way or another, I guess. I'll be obliged if you help Nancy get straightened out before you ride on."

"I don't want his help, Bud," the girl flared.

"That's temper," Bud told her. "We won't make it back to the valley on temper, Sis. If this man'll help us some, we'll do better."

The Reno Kid walked away before she could reply. He rolled a cigarette on his way to the well, and was smoking when he brought back water for the wounded men.

Meeks and Jerry got the lead oxen unyoked and the wagon dragged to the well. The Reno Kid took the lantern, examined the wounded ox, and regretfully shot it.

Next, the wounded gunman had to be bandaged and the torn bloody hole in the Reno Kid's arm tied up. Meeks reluctantly admitted to having a pint of whiskey in the wagon. The Reno Kid poured whiskey on all the wounds and saved a drink for each wounded man.

After the dead were buried in shallow graves, Meeks, at the Reno Kid's orders, carried the wounded men and prisoner to a small cook fire near the well where Nancy Willis had coffee boiling, bacon and beans hot on tin plates.

The Reno Kid drank three cups of black coffee, ate a plate of beans and bread, and then lifted the lantern and looked at the dust-covered water barrels in the wagon.

Five barrels. Filling them a bucket at a time would take hours, although a second bucket and rope were in the back of the wagon.

"Better start yanking water into those barrels," the Reno Kid decided.

Nancy challenged him across the glowing coals of the cook fire: "What good will it do? One yoke of oxen can't pull the wagon and the water back."

"Water these King horses an' give them some of that fodder you brought, and they'll help pull you back, ma'am."

"And what will Strickland King do?"

"Might be he'd thank you for bringing two of his men back."

"You're making fun of us!" she cried unsteadily. "Oh, I hate people like you and everything you stand for."

The Reno Kid lit another cigarette. His unsmiling face was somber.

"I never said what I stood for, ma'am. You've got to get back. King's men have got to get back. Might as well use the horses and take all the water you can."

Bud Willis raised up from the sand where he had been lying. "He's right, Sis. Whatever happens is going to happen anyway. We'll get back the best way and take water."

"And Strickland King will accuse us of murder, horse stealing, and anything else he can think of," Nancy said bitterly, "while this . . . this man rides away, laughing to himself."

"What he does ain't any business of ours," Bud Willis declared solidly. "King would have got us sooner or later anyway. Maybe I can sit up there in the wagon an' pour the water in the barrels."

"I'll help all I can," the Reno Kid offered. "This arm ain't too bad."

"We're not asking you for help," Nancy flashed.

"I'll just do it without being asked," the Reno Kid replied gravely.

And that was the way it was done, hour after hour of back-breaking labor, dragging dripping buckets of water out of the deep well and emptying them into the wagon barrels.

The Reno Kid's hands grew raw from holding rough wet ropes. Back and arms protested painfully at the unaccustomed exercise, sleep and weariness dragged at his eyes, and feverish pain throbbed in the wounded arm.

Three barrels were full and the fourth was partly full when the Reno Kid called a halt. "You can't haul any more," he declared. "I've got to catch some sleep and be riding after sunup. Jerry, how'd you like to buckle on a gun an' watch this tied-up *hombre?*"

"By golly, I'll watch him!" Jerry exclaimed delightedly. "Want me to shoot him if he gets dangerous?"

"You better call me if it gets to that," the Reno Kid decided gravely. "Shooting is serious business. Never touch a gun until there ain't any other way out."

Nancy flushed. "You should be ashamed putting such ideas in a boy's head. I've tried to teach Jerry to live decently and keep away from guns . . . and now you're making cowardly killers seem like heroes to him."

"Tell King that, ma'am," said the Reno Kid. "I ain't fenced in any water holes . . . and I ain't going to get loose while you're asleep and grab for a gun."

"An' this skunk ain't, either," Jerry Willis said stoutly as he buckled on a gun belt too big for his thin middle. "You git to sleep, Sis. I aim to stay decent, but no damn' skunk is gonna get a whack at you while you're asleep tonight."

"Jerry, I won't have you talking like that," Nancy said helplessly. "Swearing and . . . and. . . ."

"I'll stop swearin'," Jerry muttered. "But I'm gonna watch this skunk plenty. I won't kill him. Cross my heart."

Bud Willis was in pain, but he chuckled. "Jerry's growed up, Sis. Better let him help out. We need it."

Nancy looked helpless and angry as she turned back to the fire. The Reno Kid was smiling faintly as he looked at her, and then, sober again, he carried more fodder to his horse, and another bucket of water. When he was finished, he threw himself down with his saddle for a pillow and was asleep in a minute or two despite the pain in his arm.

IV

A gold and crimson sunrise was bursting over the gray sky when the Reno Kid awoke, got stiffly to his feet, and grimaced at the hurt in his wounded arm. Then he grinned at the sleepy youngster plodding wearily back and forth with the heavy gun belt sagging at his leg.

"Turn in, button," the Reno Kid said.

"I watched him close," Jerry said huskily. "He cussed a little an' then went to sleep. That wounded feller had to have water plenty. He ain't been asleep long. You going to leave us, mister?"

"Got to, button."

"I'd like to go along," Jerry murmured.

"Your sister'd have something to say about that."

"I reckon so," Jerry said glumly, and then he squinted. "Are you a sure enough outlaw?"

"Reward and everything," the Reno Kid said, losing his smile. "Most likely I'll get shot any day now. Folks like your sister are right in not having much use for me. Don't ever get in my shoes, button."

"I ain't a button no more," Jerry told him. "An' I like you. What's your name?"

"Slim," said the Reno Kid. "Better go to sleep. I'll wake this other King man and we'll be gone before you know it." He shook the prisoner, waited for him to open his eyes. "I'm going to untie you. Water your horse and mine, saddle 'em, and we'll be going."

Red-eyed and unbelieving, the man stared at him, first sullenly, then with a fearful expression. "Where we going?"

"I'll tell you later. Roll over while I get at these ropes. I'll be watching you close. Don't get careless."

The others woke up while the horses were being saddled. Bud Willis rolled a cigarette and silently watched the preparations for leaving.

"Both of you going?" he inquired.

The prisoner swung on him. "You know I ain't got a chance with him. He'll put a bullet in my back out there somewhere an' jump across the border, laughin' up his sleeve. What'll you say to Strickland King when he asks why you didn't stop it?"

Bud Willis touched his wounded knee.

"I'll tell him we couldn't stop it any more than we could stop you men from dragging us into this."

Nancy Willis confronted the Reno Kid: "You can't do this!" she cried fiercely. "Hasn't there been enough killing? Let the man stay here."

"He'd just make more trouble for you folks," said the Reno Kid. "With him out of the way you'll get back all right."

Dark shadows were under her eyes and her face was pale. "I wish I were a man and had a gun."

The Reno Kid smiled faintly. "I'm glad you're puny and sweet and what you are, ma'am. It'll give me something to think about."

She was angry and helpless as Jerry's shrill warning drew her startled look.

"Keep away from them gun belts! I'm watchin' you!!"

The prisoner snarled at him.

The Reno Kid chuckled. "I had a bead on him with one eye, *compañero.*"

"Take that gun belt off, Jerry, and keep away from this outlaw," Nancy Willis blazed.

Jerry sulkily unbuckled the gun belt and tossed it with the others.

But while the prisoner and the Reno Kid were eating cold beans and bread, the youngster edged close to the Reno Kid and spoke under his breath.

"Where you headin', Slim?"

"Wouldn't do to tell," the Reno Kid said from the corner of his mouth. "But after you get back to South Valley, tell your sister I'm sure sorry I worried the sweetest girl I ever seen. She wouldn't believe me now."

135

"Bet you're in love with her like all the rest of the young fellers," Jerry said hopefully.

"Maybe that's what's making me feel so bad about her," the Reno Kid decided gravely.

"Gosh," Jerry whispered with shining eyes. "Whyn't you come home with us an marry her, Slim? I'd sure like it. Havin' an outlaw in the family'd be more fun than all the trouble we been havin'."

"Better not tell her that," the Reno Kid warned. "Being an outlaw is pretty bad, button. It ain't any fun. Remember that. An' if you ever hear of me getting shot, remember it some more."

"You ain't gonna get shot. You'll be over the border an' safe by tomorrow," Jerry said with conviction. "Say, Slim, you gonna kill that skunk?"

"Nope."

"I knowed Sis was wrong," Jerry said with relief. "Maybe she'll listen to me now."

"Jerry!" Nancy called sharply. "Come over here!"

Jerry grinned understandingly at the Reno Kid as he went over to the wagon and joined his sister.

The food was down a few minutes later. The Reno Kid and his prisoner mounted.

"Them horses and ropes to the saddles will help pull you folks in," the Reno Kid said. "*Adiós*, folks."

"So long, Slim!" Jerry called. The others were silent.

The Reno Kid and his prisoner rode away from the loaded wagon in silence, away from Murphy's Well and the high raw rocks, southeast over the vast dry flats toward the border. The prisoner rode ahead sullenly, apprehensively, and only showed his surprise miles away when they turned east, and northeast toward South Valley where the homesteaders had settled.

"Where we going?" he demanded over his shoulder.

"I'll do the talking when it's time," the Reno Kid said shortly.

"Keep riding."

South Valley was some ten miles wide. Low barren hills on the west, low mountains on the east were covered with cedar, piñon, and scattered larger timber. There had been good grass in South Valley, grass in the timbered hills and mountains to the east, water in South Creek the year around. And not a fence between Canfield and the border.

Now barbed wire was strung on gnarled fence posts. Windmills topped wells. Plows had gashed the brown earth. Small adobe houses could be seen huddling near the cottonwoods that fringed the bends of South Creek, where a road north to Canfield had been rutted out by travel.

The homesteaders had worked hard to make the land fertile and crop-yielding, and the drought had struck back hard. Plowed furrows had baked to dust under the burned-out remnants of the last crop that hadn't been worth gathering.

A few crowbait horses, bony cows, and listless sheep were visible as the two riders angled across the valley toward the road ruts and the creek. Doors were open, windows gaped, life was gone from the first two houses he passed. And when he reached the road ruts, dry white sand lay on South Creek where water had always run.

Two unshaven men in patched overalls sat listlessly on boxes before the next adobe house. They stared with hostility as the Reno Kid called: "Got a little water to spare?"

"Nope," was the surly reply.

"Where's the Willis place?"

"Dunno."

Children's heads peered fearfully out the front door as the Reno Kid and his prisoner rode on. You could almost feel the hate for cowmen, for any gun-toting riders who might be Strickland King's men.

There were other abandoned shacks, and other families clinging stubbornly to the land. All of these people stared silently as the two riders passed north up the valley. The afternoon heat was about them. The white dry sands of South Creek might have been the ghostly bones of wasted labor and dead hopes.

By legally fencing all his water holes and damming back the Big Spring that was the source of the East Fork, Strickland King had whipped the settlers. But not all of them. Somewhere back there in the west, on the sun-scorched road through Dry Bone Flat, would be a lumbering wagon carrying fierce courage with its load of water. Carrying Nancy Willis, young and lovely in her defiance.

At the north end of the valley, the Reno Kid drew rein.

"We fork here," he told his prisoner without emotion. "Tell Strickland King that Slim Considine is back. He'll be waiting to hear what luck you men had."

The sullen prisoner had become more puzzled each hour of the long day. Now he sat for a moment in scowling disbelief.

"Sure you ain't saving a bullet for my back when I start?" he wanted to know.

"It'd be a pleasure. But I ain't. Don't sit there tempting me."

The King man spurred his jaded horse toward the north, looking back over his shoulder apprehensively until he was out of gunshot range.

The Reno Kid followed the road ruts to the northeast out of the valley, through the rocky Bottleneck and the broken hills beyond, to Canfield, where the adobe houses pressed close on narrow little streets and tall cottonwoods stood around the little brick courthouse and its dusty plaza.

Canfield had not changed. Dogs barked, windows showed lights in the evening darkness, horses stood at the plaza hitch racks. In the country beyond Canfield were cattle and mines, lumber and trade. Water, too, and reserves and strength against drought.

The Reno Kid's horse could not have traveled much farther when his rider dismounted before a small dark building on the north side of the plaza and stopped a passing man. "Know where Lawyer Jackson might be?" he asked.

"Jupe's havin' a few drinks at the Owlhead, I reckon. He mostly is this time of the evening."

"Mind stopping at the Owlhead and telling him he's got a customer?"

The door of Jupe Jackson's office was unlocked. The Reno Kid stepped to the back corner of the front room, and grinned when he encountered a tin bucket of drinking water and a long-handled dipper. It felt like the same old battered bucket and dipper. He drank thirstily, rolled a cigarette, and was seated on a table edge holding his Winchester when a short man smelling of cloves and rye came in, struck a match to light a lamp, and said briskly: "Want to see me?"

"Sort of," the Reno Kid replied without moving. "I'm Slim Considine. How in hell do you come to be leasing the Cold Spring land to Strickland King?"

The lamp chimney shattered on the floor as the small man jumped around. "Great Jupiter! Young Considine!"

V

Jupe Jackson hurriedly blew out the smoking lamp wick. The light had shown his white hair, alert face, wiry frame in a neat black suit.

"The back room'll be better," he suggested nervously. "There are men in town who know you."

"And could use a reward," the Reno Kid added, rising.

"Two thousand, dead or alive. Never been withdrawn. But that isn't all," Jupe Jackson said nervously. "Long Tom Simms, who ramrods for King, was in town yesterday. He said one of their old men just rode in from Dakota, saying he recognized you up north using another name and handy with your guns."

"The Reno Kid?"

"Well . . . yes." Jupe Jackson cleared his throat. "The man said you left there on the run, after a fight with peace officers."

"I guessed it was someone from around here who read my sign to those Dakota lawmen," the Reno Kid said thoughtfully. "Two thousand reward made 'em reckless. There was shooting before I got away. What about this Strickland King lease?"

"Come in the back room," Jupe Jackson urged. He pulled the back-room window shades down, turned a key in the back door, and locked the other door before he lit another lamp.

The Reno Kid squinted unsmilingly at the older man's face. Jupe Jackson opened a desk drawer and set out a bottle and glasses. "Drink?"

"Thanks."

Jupe Jackson gulped a drink at the same time and smiled wryly as he sat in an old high-back desk chair that seemed to swallow him.

"You gave me a turn, Considine, speaking out in the dark that way. Now about Cold Spring. Your father had just died and you and your brother were the heirs. Then your brother was shot and you took it on the run out of here."

"With a posse of Strickland King's men after me and Strickland King's money guaranteeing the reward he got plastered on me for being a kid with guts enough to shoot back when him and his men gunned Dave down."

"King's witnesses had a story about that which put you and your brother in the wrong," Jupe Jackson said. "Doubtless you have another. The law would have to pass on both stories and any proof. You were under age at the time. Your father's estate hadn't been settled and turned over to you and your brother. So when you vanished, there was nothing for the court to do but appoint a trustee. Judge Maxon appointed me. And, as

trustee, I sold your cattle at a good price and leased the property
to Strickland King at the highest price I could get out of him."
The lawyer reached for the bottle again. "I made a good trade.
King was expanding and needed your water rights."

"A hell of a trade," the Reno Kid said curtly. "You leased my
land to the skunk who gunned my brother and lied about it and
slapped a dead or alive reward on me."

"That's right," agreed Jupe Jackson briskly. "I don't mix my
feelings in other folk's trouble. Never have and never will. It's
bad enough to be their lawyer. I was your trustee with a duty to
make the best out of your land. I took the highest offer I could
get. King wanted to buy the place. He's ranted and raised hell
ever since to make me sell the place instead of lease. Said you'd
never be back here, and, if you did come back, you'd be hung
for killing one of his men and he might as well buy the place
now as later. I even went so far as to put a clause in the lease,
that, if and when you came back and disapproved of the lease, it
was void on your say-so. And there's a large sum of money in
the bank to your credit. Outlaw or no outlaw, the ranch and the
money are yours. Court isn't sitting now, but all the papers can
be signed quickly. The rest is up to you."

"I was too hasty," the Reno Kid admitted. "I thought maybe
you were playing King's game."

Jupe Jackson clasped his hands behind his head and spoke
tolerantly. "I can't stop any man from being a damned fool."

"King's lease is busted from now on," the Reno Kid said. "I
want his stock off the land quick. Pull out your pen and draw
up a lease turning the land over to a lady named Nancy Willis,
who lives in South Valley. And then write a will giving her the
land to keep if I'm killed, hung, shot, or don't get word back for
two years. The lease to run until I stop it. Dollar a year rent."

Jupe Jackson poured a big drink of whiskey and gulped it
down.

"Son, you got any idea how much hell all this will turn loose around here?" he asked finally.

"It's legal, isn't it?"

"Great Jupiter, it's too legal," Jackson said in almost a groan. "Strickland King won't be able to law about it. He'll have to take matters into his own hands. You must know this Willis girl is one of the homesteaders in South Valley. There's been trouble enough about them . . . and this will blow everything up. Strickland King won't take it lying down."

"He likes his legal rights. This'll be something legal for him to chew on."

"You like the lady, I gather?" said Jackson.

"I didn't say so."

The lawyer reached for a handkerchief and mopped his forehead.

"Bound to like her or you wouldn't be doing all this. But, son, you aren't doing her any favors. Strickland King's caught with too many cattle in a drought year and short on water anyway. With you outlawed and a reward on your head, you won't be around. But Miss Willis will be, and what do you suppose King will do about her when he finds she's got his lease? Not to speak of what he might do if he found out she was due to inherit the land? After the homesteaders are run out, King intends to throw cattle in South Valley again. He's said so. This will cut him off to the south for good. You're making bad trouble for that girl."

"She's got trouble enough already, hauling water forty miles each way with ox teams," the Reno Kid said doggedly. "Ever since I left here I've been getting ready to come back and prove it was Long Tom Simms and those other King men who picked a quarrel with Dave that day. Dave and I shot in self-defense. I don't know which one of us killed the King man. When the lawmen up in Dakota tried to arrest me, I knew the reward was still on me and I might as well come back and find out the truth."

"Not much chance of ever doing that," Jackson stated. "You and your brother killed one of those King men. Brady Mahon, the other man who signed the charge against you, is dead. That means Long Tom Simms is the only one left who knows whether or not it was self-defense."

"I figured someone knew the truth," the Reno Kid said. "So I came back. I stopped at the Stinking Rocks for water and two King riders came along. One of them recognized me and started shooting. I crippled him. The other got away. I decided to drop down across the border and wait until things quieted down. But the man who got away met three other King men and they rode after me. Followed me all day yesterday out across Dry Bone Flat to Murphy's Well. And last night they snuck up on me under cover of the wagon the Willis girl and her brothers had driven out there to load with water. It was dark and every man for himself when they opened fire on me. I killed two of them, shot another pretty bad, and tied the fourth man up. He's going to swear Miss Willis and her bunch helped me. King will back him up."

"Great Jupiter. Homesteaders, too. They'd better head out of these parts."

"They're bringing the wounded man back in the wagon," the Reno Kid told him. "I rode ahead with the other one and turned him loose to tell King I was back. He'll be after me before he takes time to bother with those homesteaders. What kind of a sheriff is Tobe Barrett?"

"A good one in a hard job," Jackson said. "Strickland King wants a bootlicking sheriff and Tobe won't lick. I'm looking for King to try to get another man elected next year."

"Can your law protect Miss Willis?"

The lawyer shrugged. "Judge Meachem will back up Tobe

Barrett. No one wanted those homesteaders over in South Valley, not the cattle folks, anyway. But the way Strickland King has barred them from water has made folks sorry for them. Part of the town wells are dry. Not enough water around here to help them. Who's going to help you, Considine, when Strickland King comes roaring in with his gunmen to make sure you're arrested and shot or hanged? Which he'll do. He furnished the reward money in the first place. It's still on deposit."

"I'll take my chances with King and his gunmen."

Jackson drummed lightly on the chair arm as he frowned thoughtfully. "Tobe Barrett might lock you up until you can stand trial legally."

"Hell of a chance I'd have cooped up in jail with Strickland King on the outside dead set to have me shot or hanged."

"Speaking as a lawyer, I'd give you about an even chance," conceded Jackson. "But as a man who's watched Strickland King for more than twenty years, I wouldn't give you one damned bit of a chance. He talks law when it suits him and he'd have a friend shot in the back if it fitted his plans. My advice to you is to leave until things quiet down. Maybe I can do something for you later on."

The Reno Kid smiled. "Good advice. Worth every cent you charge. And while I have my hide, King wipes out those homesteaders. I'm not a homesteader starving for water, or a kid on a range road not sure what to do when King's men pull guns. I'm back. I'll stay. I need a bite to eat and a fresh horse. Does a trustee's duties take in that much service?"

"The court doesn't authorize a trustee to help a man defy the law," said Jupe Jackson briefly. "I'll make out the necessary papers while you're here and you can sign them."

The dry little lawyer selected a clean pen, fresh paper, and began to write rapidly. When papers were made out and signed, he swung his chair around.

"I never did think Dave Considine and his kid brother opened fire on three King men, no matter what was sworn to," he said unemotionally. "Other people didn't, either. But the law is the law. You rode off and stayed away. That may hang you yet."

"I rode to keep from being left there in the road with Dave. Then I heard of the reward. I stayed away until I was man enough to meet it."

Jackson peered up, muttering in a low voice: "You're young, reckless . . . other folks' troubles on your mind, too. You'll stay here now and get shot. Jupiter," he stood up hastily. "Can't help you as a trustee, son. But I can take your case as a lawyer."

The Reno Kid smiled faintly and patted the Winchester cradled in his arm and the holstered gun at his side. "I brought two lawyers along."

"Strickland King will match you five to one and raise you," Jackson said dryly. "He'd like it that way. A good lawyer won't get you shot any quicker than making a hot-headed stand against King."

"All right, you're hired. Now what?"

Jupe Jackson tossed down another drink and considered.

"I'll take your horse to the livery stable and buy you another in case you have to leave town quickly. Wait here. And put out that light." The Reno Kid obeyed and Jackson closed the door behind him.

The dark office was quiet. The Reno Kid went into the front room for more water. Through the window he could see two horsemen cantering toward the plaza. King's gunmen would be riding the night now. And out there west of the valley Nancy Willis would be coming home with her precious water. The lawyer was right. King would destroy the Willises if necessary.

Once a passing man looked into the dark office and went on. He'd hurry to the sheriff if he knew who stood in the dark

145

room. A $2,000 reward was a mighty big incentive to a man to play bounty hunter. Crafty of Strickland King to keep the reward in force. Dead or alive. No man was safe with that over his head.

A rider dismounted outside. The Reno Kid waited, hand on his gun. Jupe Jackson came quickly into the dark office.

"There's your horse out there," the lawyer said. "Ride over to my house and eat while we plan what to do."

"Should have hired you years ago." The Reno Kid chuckled as he preceded Jackson out the front door. Then he stopped short.

Two men jumped him from the sides of the doorway where they had been waiting. The Kid tried to dodge back and reach his gun. Jupe Jackson blocked him. The lawyer caught his arms from behind, hampered him for the second it took the others to seize his arms.

VI

"You're arrested, Considine," Jackson warned. "Don't make me shoot you. Hold him, Perea."

"*¡Caramba!* He's damn' wil'cat."

"I've got his Colt," Jupe Jackson panted.

"I might've known a crooked lawyer would trick me," the Reno Kid raged as a gun muzzle dug in his left side. "Easy with that left arm. It's wounded!"

Handcuffs locked his wrists. The Winchester was snatched away.

"Bring him inside," Jackson ordered. "I want a receipt for him, Barrett."

"You'll get the reward all right, I guess, Jackson."

"I'll make sure. King is tricky."

"Not as tricky as a dirty lawyer who takes a man's case and then turns him over to the sheriff," the Reno Kid growled as they hustled him in the back room.

Jupe Jackson lit the lamp again and hurriedly scrawled a few lines on a sheet of paper.

Tobe Barrett, the sheriff, was a leathery old-timer with a black mustache, calfskin vest, and weathered Stetson. Blue eyes were cold in his seamed face as he turned the prisoner over to his Mexican deputy.

Barrett's voice, too, was cold as he signed the paper.

"The law wants him an' I'm takin' him. But damned if I like the way I got him."

Jupe Jackson's white hair was bristling; his smile was satisfied as he pocketed the receipt for the prisoner.

"It was my duty to have him arrested. He'd have been shot anyway, sooner or later."

"An' you wouldn't have had two thousand in your britches," Tobe Barrett reminded coldly. "Come along, Considine. Watch him close, Ricardo. He won't take this kindly."

"Don't shoot unless you have to, Perea," Jupe Jackson urged piously.

Ricardo Perea eyed the brisk little lawyer. "Reward ees dead or alive, no? W'at you care? Come, *hombre.*"

Jupe Jackson walked briskly ahead of them.

"Makin' damn' sure of his reward," Tobe Barrett muttered. "It's gettin' so a man can trust nobody any more. Considine, I knowed your brother. I'm sorry about this."

"Thanks, Sheriff."

A passing man stopped, stared, turned back to follow them.

Two more men fell in to see what was happening. They came to the Owlhead Saloon, a deep, low-roofed adobe building with a long bar, the most popular drinking place in Canfield. Horses were at the Owlhead rack, voices and laughter inside, as Jupe Jackson pushed aside one of the swinging doors and looked inside.

"Judge Meachem's in here, Sheriff. I'd like him to see the prisoner. My treat, too, I guess."

"Someone else'll drink up your dirty reward money," Tobe Barrett said shortly. "The judge oughta see the prisoner an' hear what you done. Next time court sits he'll know what kind of a lawyer he's got in front of him."

A dozen or more men at the bar and tables turned to stare as the sheriff and his deputy brought the handcuffed prisoner in behind Jupe Jackson.

The Reno Kid remembered something of the white-haired, pink-faced shrewdness of old Judge Meachem, who ran his terms of court with an iron hand. Now the judge turned from the bar with a glass of whiskey in his hand.

"Good evening, Jackson. 'Evening, Sheriff. What's this?"

"Young feller named Considine, Judge," Tobe Barrett said. "Charge of shootin' one of Strickland King's men five, six years ago. King put up a reward."

"*Hm-m-m.* Yes, I remember." Judge Meachem nodded. "Two thousand dollars reward, wasn't it? I believe the money is still on deposit." The judge tossed off his drink and wiped his white mustache. "Good work, Barrett. A tidy little nest egg for you and your deputy."

Jupe Jackson took a folded paper from his coat pocket.

"Here's the sheriff's receipt for the prisoner, judge . . . made out to me. I get the reward. The sheriff acted on my information."

A grizzled cowman spoke from among the spectators: "You oughta get a bullwhip on your back, Jackson. I knowed his father and brother and him. Anybody they ever kilt had it cumin' to him."

That was old Pete Morrison, who had punched cows on the home ranch long years back.

"Thanks, Pete," the Reno Kid said. "But this is the law now.

148

Jackson's kind of law. Strickland King's law."

Judge Meachem nodded as he returned the paper to Jupe Jackson.

"You're entitled to the reward, Jackson. And, gentlemen, the law deserves respect. I'll not hear otherwise."

The Reno Kid grinned mirthlessly. "Tell it to Strickland King. When I hear law after this, I'll look for a smooth-talking hypocrite."

Jackson cleared his throat. "Judge, I'm counsel for this prisoner."

"Like hell you are!" the Reno Kid exploded.

"And," Jackson continued calmly, "I'd like to ask the court to order the prisoner released on bail. Evidence of murder isn't conclusive. The prisoner's return shows good faith. The hard-pressed taxpayers shouldn't support the prisoner in idleness until the next term of court. In my opinion a large cash bail, which we are prepared to furnish, will meet the legal requirements."

"A very convincing argument, Mister Jackson," Judge Meachem said solemnly. He poured another drink and cleared his throat. "I'll have to insist on a large cash bail, Mister Jackson. Nothing under two thousand dollars would be satisfactory."

"I suggest, Judge, that the court take over the two thousand reward, which is on deposit anyway, and hold the money as bail."

"*Hm-m-m,*" said Judge Meachem. "Well, Mister Jackson, since the money is on deposit, I don't see why it won't serve. Sheriff, the prisoner is admitted to bail. The court orders you to see that no one hinders the prisoner from presenting his person to the court on order."

Pete Morrison let out a whoop.

"Drinks on me, gentlemen!" Jupe Jackson called.

Tobe Barrett looked dazed as he unlocked the handcuffs. "It don't sound right, but I reckon it is if the judge says so. Usin' Strickland King's reward money to set you free. Might have knowed Jupe had somethin' besides a dirty trick up his sleeve."

The Reno Kid caught Jupe Jackson's arm. "You had this all figured out," he accused huskily.

Jupe Jackson winked and answered from the corner of his mouth: "All you needed was a good lawyer. I had to get you arrested to keep the sheriff from helping Strickland King hunt you down tonight. I saw the judge while I was buying you a horse and he allowed I was right. Now all you've got to do is keep away from Strickland King's gunmen while we figure a way to meet that murder charge. We. . . ."

"Horses!" the Reno Kid said, and turned, listening, the smile fading from his face.

"Here comes some more to hear the news!" Pete Morrison yelled gleefully. "I'd shore like to see the look on Strickland King's face when he hears what his damn' reward done!"

One of the men had stepped to the swinging doors and looked out as riders stopped at the hitch rack out front. He spoke dryly over his shoulder: "You're gonna see, Morrison. These are King men . . . an', by Jupiter, King an' his *segundo,* Tom Simms, are along."

Jupe Jackson caught the Reno Kid's right wrist. "Slip out the back way. This isn't any place for you now."

"You've made it as good a place as any." The Reno Kid put his back to the bar. His face went bleak and without expression as he waited.

Hurried and dusty, they surged in through the swinging doors, eight of them, carrying rifles and side guns. The first were noisy for drinks as they made for the bar. The two last men in through the swinging doors were Long Tom Simms and Strickland King.

Simms looked the same as he always had to the Reno Kid's narrowed eyes. Long and lean, with corded neck muscles, a hard tight mouth and drooping eyelids that made him look deceptive and slow. And a way of smiling that was friendly at times—until a man learned that Long Tom Simms had no friend but himself.

Strickland King was taller by an inch, gray in his black hair now, eyes cold and bleak in a face that was as arrogant as the set of his shoulders and the walk of him in expensive riding boots into which gray trousers were tucked. His gray coat, open in front, showed the pearl-handled revolver underneath, and the gray silk neckerchief was held by a massive gold tie ring. His eyes were watchful on the room as Long Tom Simms called: "Sheriff, we want you! There's an outlaw loose around here! That young Considine, who shot Joey Byers six years ago. He killed some more of our men last night and we're out to get him this time."

"Don't know anything about all that," Tobe Barrett drawled. "The man's been arrested on that old charge. Jupe Jackson here gets the reward."

"Jackson gets the reward?" Strickland King broke in, elbowing past his men. A sneer broke over his face. "Know how to look out for yourself, eh, Jackson? Well, you'll get the money."

"He'd better," Judge Meachem said blandly. "The court's accepted the reward money as bail for young Considine. We'll hear all the evidence at the trial."

The sheriff was standing in front of the Reno Kid, half hiding him from King and his men. But past Barrett's shoulder there was no trouble in seeing the quick flush of rage on King's face.

"Meachem, did you take *my* reward money and let that damn' young killer go free?"

Judge Meachem was cold in his answer. "The prisoner's lawyer prevailed on the court to admit the prisoner to bail."

"Who's the lawyer who argued you into a fool move like that?" Strickland King raged.

"Jackson represented the prisoner. You're pretty close to contempt of court in your language." Judge Meachem poured himself another drink.

Strickland King sounded as if he were near to choking. "Jackson just admitted having him arrested."

Jupe Jackson regarded the bigger man solemnly. "I did my lawful duty and had Considine arrested. And then, as Considine's lawyer, I argued bail. Everything's legal. No need for you to worry."

"Legal!" Strickland King said violently. "You want everything legal, do you? What about those other two men of mine that that young gunman killed last night?"

"Two sides to that," said Jupe Jackson. "I'll demand witnesses."

"You'll get 'em!"

"Don't bother the lady and her brothers," the Reno Kid said softly past the sheriff's shoulder.

Strickland King looked to see who had spoken. Tobe Barrett moved and Long Tom Simms yelled: "That's him standin' there all the time! He's growed up, but that's him!"

Simms was streaking for his gun as he spoke. But the Reno Kid's rifle muzzle had already tipped forward ready for a shot and the sheriff drew fast, also.

"None of that!" Barrett warned. "The young feller's out on bail an' protected by the law! Ricardo, watch those men!"

"I watch heem," the deputy said stolidly over his gun.

The other King men hadn't recognized the Reno Kid until it was too late to draw. They shuffled uneasily, waiting for a command.

Judge Meachem set his empty glass down carefully as Long Tom Simms slowly held his hands waist high. The other men had hastily moved away from the guns and were watching tensely to see what would happen.

In the moment of quiet the Reno Kid spoke softly: "I'm back, King. Tear up that lease on my land, and get your cattle off."

Strickland King had gone immobile again. Angry fires were blazing in his eyes, but he was calm and icy.

"You seem to have all the law on your side, Considine. But I'm a law-abiding man. Simms, I don't want any more trouble over this. Bring the men over to the Buckhorn Bar. We'll let the law handle everything."

Strickland King walked out of the saloon, a tall, gray, icy man with hellfire still glowing in his eyes. Long Tom Simms gave the Reno Kid a scowl and led the other King men out.

"Barkeep, gimme a double rye!" one of the spectators said explosively. "That was too close for comfort."

Jupe Jackson plucked at the Reno Kid's sleeve.

"Come over to my house and let the doctor fix that arm, and get some sleep while you can. And it isn't too late to ride like hell and hide out until I send you word."

"Everything's legal and settled, ain't it?"

"Everything but killing you off," Jupe Jackson told him. "That'll take just as long as King needs to make plans. He knows where he stands now, and what he's got to do."

"I thought so." The Reno Kid nodded. "He's not gunning for me right under the sheriff's and the judge's noses, but he knew what he was going to do when he went out of here."

"What?"

"I don't know," said the Reno Kid. "And I don't aim to sit around until King shows me. I'll take it kindly if you'll send the doctor to South Valley to meet the Willis wagon. My arm stopped bleeding long ago. It can wait a little. I'll take a bite of the free lunch and go about my business."

"Don't do anything foolish," the white-haired little lawyer

pleaded. "I did the best I could, but you're only out on bail, son. Don't give King a chance to say you set out looking for trouble right away. It'll look bad."

"I'll look worse if I let King snap a trap on me, mister."

VII

The Reno Kid slipped out of the back door of the Owlhead and once more became a part of the dark night. Only now it was different. He had found men who weren't after blood money, men who wouldn't jump at Strickland King's bidding.

But there was still Strickland King to reckon with, and the men he *had* been able to buy.

Jupe Jackson had procured a long-legged, powerful sorrel. The Reno Kid rode the horse to a hitch rack at the end of the plaza. Here he was a stranger in the shadows as he skirted on around the plaza on foot.

King and his men were in the Buckhorn Bar just ahead. Long Tom Simms was in there. Simms had cold-bloodedly triggered Dave Considine to death six years back and would as callously swear on the witness stand that Dave and his kid brother had started the trouble.

The Reno Kid stepped into a dark doorway as men came out of the Buckhorn and forked horses at the rack.

"Bring the doctor to the Big Spring by sunrise," Strickland King's voice said. "If Tex is still alive when the boys get him there, I want him pulled through if we have to light a fire under the devil. And keep away from Considine."

They left the plaza fast, riding west out of town. The two men left behind went back into the Buckhorn. The Reno Kid stepped out of the doorway and saw the two in the door light. Long Tom Simms had ridden off with King.

Over near the Owlhead a Chinese served meals. The Reno Kid crossed there and ordered ham and eggs and black coffee.

He felt better as he followed the Chinaman's directions to the doctor's house.

Old Doc Thomas, he found, was dead. The new doctor was a young man from the East, earnest and concerned about a man who had been shot.

"I'll put your arm in a sling and you'd better go to bed for a day or so," he said briskly as he finished dressing the arm.

"Sure, Doc," the Reno Kid assented amiably, and, when he was outside on the fresh horse, he threw the sling away and rode west out of town. West, toward the Big Spring Ranch, through country the night could not hide. As a boy, Slim Considine had known every mile of this country. And now the Reno Kid, branded as a killer by Strickland King, had come back and was riding home.

The ranch house had been adobe, with a bunkhouse and corrals. The low ridges around the spot were studded with rock outcrops, patches of brush, and gnarled trees.

The Big Spring boiled from the ledges at the foot of a rocky ridge. Some said it was a natural spring, some said it was the water of Blind Creek that vanished twenty-odd miles to the north after rushing out of the mountains.

But the Big Spring water had never failed. Tonight there was water in the Big Spring, and water backed up in the draws half a mile below the spring.

Strickland King had thrown a dam between two rocky ridges that pinched together where the water channel passed toward South Creek. The area behind the dam he had fenced in. The night outside the fence was uneasy with hundreds of restless cattle that waited to be admitted to the water.

A match flared off to the left about where the dam would be. King had guards there. The dry hoof-packed ground, the fence and water beyond, and the number of cattle told the story.

King was using the Big Spring flow for his main water, moving cattle in from his own drought-afflicted range. Take the Big Spring away now at the height of the drought and Strickland King would be close to ruin.

But if the Big Spring water was kept from the homesteaders, they would be driven out of South Valley, and no man between the mountains and the border would be as strong as Strickland King.

Looking back now, it was possible to see how Strickland King had planned all this through twenty years and more. Buying a man out here, crowding a man out there, cold-bloodedly moving step by step toward his goal.

Dave Considine's murder had been one step. Dave's kid brother had not mattered much in King's plans. The reward should have taken care of him.

But the reward hadn't worked. Judge Meachem and Jupe Jackson had kept the law straight in the matter of the Big Spring ownership.

Government law had let the homesteaders in South Valley. Drought and Strickland King had almost settled that problem. Only the courage of Nancy Willis and a few others like her held out now against King.

The Reno Kid was thoughtful as he rode back from the fenced-in water. King would lose half a lifetime of planning if he lost the Big Spring now. He'd fight to hold it. Killing wouldn't matter. King's face had told that when he stalked out of the Owlhead back there in Canfield.

King was up to something tonight. The wounded man he wanted doctored must be the man Nancy Willis was bringing in. That meant King had sent men riding fast to meet the homesteader's wagon.

They were bringing the man here, the nearest point to South Valley. King wanted him to live at all costs. Some trick King was planning suited him better than ordering his men out on a gun hunt after the Reno Kid.

Midnight was long past. The Reno Kid had ridden leisurely from Canfield, favoring his horse, fighting to keep awake and stand the pain in his swollen, feverish arm. Fatigue made each movement an effort. Bloodshot eyes closed and smarted even in the dark. But while night masked his movements, there was time to find out what King was up to. The doctor wasn't due yet and they wouldn't be expecting the Reno Kid out here tonight.

A yellow patch of light marked a window of the old ranch house. The Reno Kid rode easily beyond the next ridge, tied the reins to a cedar branch, and crossed the ridge on foot toward the back of the house.

His pockets still bulged with the cartridges he had brought from Murphy's Well; the smooth barrel of the Winchester was cool in his hand. The night wind, whispering in the cedars and brush, covered the slight sound of his advance.

Off in the south a gunshot snapped, thin and clear, on the night. A moment later a rider galloped south from the house. There were no more shots.

Puzzled, the Reno Kid sat on the ground and waited. In a little while he heard several other riders returning. Then the rattle of wheels that came to the front of the house had stopped.

That would be the wounded man Nancy Willis had been bringing home. Men were talking at the front of the house when the Reno Kid reached the back.

"Put him on the floor," Strickland King's voice said impatiently. "He'll be all right. Bring those damned nesters in."

Then a man swore out in front. "I'll break your neck if you bite me again, you little rattler!"

Jerry Willis's shrill reply trembled with anger. "If I had me a gun, I'd show you! Leggo my sister's arm!"

"Jerry! Please be quiet!"

That was Nancy Willis, weary, close to tears, if the sound of her voice was any indication.

Jerry was close to tears, too. "Callin' us horse thieves an' killers an' takin' us away from our wagon like we was headed for a lynchin'! If Slim'd been there, we'd 'a' kilt a couple more!"

Bud Willis spoke curtly. "Shut up, Jerry!"

The old adobe ranch house had weathered badly. Glass in the back windows was broken. Light gleamed through a partly opened door into the front room and Strickland King's cold voice was clear.

"The boy isn't telling us anything we don't know. My men tell me you were caught using two of our horses, which makes you horse thieves in any cow country. You sided with an outlaw and helped kill two of my men."

"They oughta all been kilt," Jerry gulped.

"Jerry," Nancy said angrily. And she answered King as angrily: "You know that isn't so. Your men took possession of our wagon and slipped up to Murphy's Well in the dark pretending to be our party. They started shooting without warning. Everything that happened to them was their own fault. Two of our oxen were shot at the same time. We had to use your horses. We were bringing them back to you."

"Thieving homesteaders weren't wanted in these parts in the first place," Strickland King continued in the same cold voice. "Those that had good sense moved out. You there, by the wall. What's your name?"

"Name of Meeks," was the mumbled reply.

"A hang rope will stretch that scrawny neck longer if I don't get the truth out of you."

The Reno Kid could almost see the hard-faced gunmen standing in there, and the gray threat of Strickland King's face. Like death itself to a drought-whipped homesteader more used to plow reins than to guns.

"Ain't any reason why I wouldn't tell the truth," Meeks answered huskily.

"I want the truth that you'll swear to in court against that young killer who's under arrest in Canfield," King said metallically. "And if I get the truth, I'll see that you're on your feet again with an outfit and money to get out of these parts and start over in better shape somewhere else. That goes for all of you. This outlaw shot my men as soon as he learned who they were. Shot them down in cold blood."

"No!" Nancy cried. "Your men shot first."

Strickland King ignored her. "Meeks, you were there. What's the truth, damn you?"

VIII

The nester was silent for a moment. Then he faltered: "Hit was dark. A man couldn't see much. Mighta been the way you say."

"You'd swear that in court?"

"I reckon so."

"You're a worse coward than I thought, Meeks," Nancy Willis said fiercely.

"I've got kids an' the old woman waitin' with no water nor much food," the nester mumbled. "All I aim to do is get home an' mind my business. If I seen somethin', I seen it."

"You won't regret it, mister," Strickland King promised. "Tex here will swear the same. So will his partner who got away before Considine could kill him."

"You're a liar!" Jerry cried shrilly. "Slim promised he wasn't goin' to kill that skunk! I wisht . . . !"

There was a slap and the sound of someone falling. "Keep your mouth shut or you'll get worse," growled a voice that sounded like Long Tom Simms.

"Brave men," Nancy blazed. "What else can you think of?"

"Horse thieves and killers," Strickland King told her,

unmoved. "You've got your last chance to tell the truth about that young killer."

"You heard us," drawled Bud.

"I heard you," said Strickland King. "And I'm wondering what your sister will do if something happens to you tonight. Men in these parts make short work of nesters who steal horses and mix in gun trouble. After I leave you, I can't stop anything that may happen."

"Bud, he means it," Nancy gasped.

"Nesters find plenty o' trouble in cow country," Long Tom Simms sneered.

"A doctor is coming here," King informed them. "That leg could be fixed and you'd have no more worries."

"Listening to a skunk like you worries me," Bud Willis assured him calmly.

Baffled rage colored Strickland King's voice for the first time.

"Simms, I'm riding back to the ranch. I don't want any trouble with the law. We've got proof that'll hang Considine. Let the lady and her brothers go."

"We'll give 'em hosses to ride home," Simms told him stolidly. "What happens after that ain't any of our business."

The Reno Kid was skirting the house when he beard Strickland King's reply. "The law will handle everything. I wash my hands of the matter."

A four-horse team, a light wagon, and half a dozen saddle horses were standing in front of the house as Strickland King strode out to the big bay he had ridden from Canfield. There was a gun pressing into King's back before he knew what was happening.

"Reach," said the Reno Kid.

King dropped the reins and obeyed. The Reno Kid shoved him around for a shield as Simms came out of the house.

"What the hell!" Simms exclaimed loudly as he saw King facing him with lifted arms. Then Simms clawed for his gun and yelled as he dodged back against the man following him out of the doorway. "Trouble out here! Git out the back way!"

"Stop them, King," the Reno Kid ordered.

"Considine's got a gun in my back!" Strickland King said in a strangled voice. "Wait, men!"

Simms had dodged over to one side of the doorway. The man behind him had ducked back into the house. Through the window the Reno Kid glimpsed several others breaking for the back door. King's shout brought quiet for a moment, and in that moment the Reno Kid's harsh words carried.

"You cut bait for a killer an' got him! King and I are taking the homesteaders to Canfield in the wagon! Better warn 'em to keep out of it, King. Tell 'em to hand their guns an' belts over and keep outta this!"

"Slim!" Jerry Willis shrieked.

"Simms, he'll do it!" Strickland King cried in a strangled voice. "Handle your men!"

"Boys, you heard it!" Simms called harshly. "Shuck your guns out here."

"There's only one feller got King!" a man called incredulously from the corner of the house.

"One's enough," the Reno Kid said. "Move fast!"

Long Tom Simms sounded baffled. "Come out, men, an' get it over with."

Two of them came, scowling and unwilling, out the front door. The Reno Kid couldn't see the men who had dashed out the back way. He looked for them while he kept a watchful eye on King and the men by the doorway.

There were seven or eight around at least, and others down by the dam. Hard men, gun-hungry for a chance at the lone stranger who had tricked them. Chances were they'd try something before the wagon got to Canfield. The Reno Kid

161

knew he'd been a fool to try this, but there hadn't been anything else to do.

"Back toward the wagon," he told his prisoner—and, as they moved, a rifle shot crashed out beyond the end of the house where one of King men had circled.

A shock on the right shoulder made the Reno Kid lurch. They'd tricked him, after all. And now not even King's death would do much to help Nancy and her brothers.

King was shrinking away as the Reno kid started to squeeze the trigger. And then the scream that came from Strickland King froze the Kid's finger before he could shoot. Like nothing human, that scream. And King wasn't shrinking away; he was falling like a log of wood with the scream trailing off as he landed heavily and groveled.

"King's shot!" Simms bawled as the Reno Kid dived past the body toward the lighted door.

The rifle spoke again and missed.

A gun licked fire from the spot where Simm's voice still echoed, and the Reno Kid's six-gun was already crashing at the spot.

Death had caught Simms and the two men out front by surprise. They scattered from the Reno Kid's blasting gun. Other guns out in the night opened up and the Reno Kid ran a gauntlet of screaming lead to the door. A bullet wrenched the brim of his sombrero, another grazed the back of his shoulder, and the last shot roared from the Colt as he hurled himself through the doorway, calling: "Put out the light!"

He glimpsed the wounded man on the floor, along with Meeks, Bud, and Jerry. Nancy Willis was darting to the oil lamp in the wall bracket. He slammed the door as the light went out, and the back room door banged shut an instant later.

Jerry's voice broke with excitement from the back of the room. "I closed this door, Slim! Gimme a gun!"

The Reno Kid jumped aside as lead splintered through the front-door planks.

"Jerry, get your sister down on the floor," he ordered.

"What happened out there?" asked Bud Willis.

"They tried to gun me in the dark an' hit King in the back instead," the Reno Kid panted as he finished reloading the six-gun. "Can you stand and use this rifle?"

Nancy Willis spoke beside him. "Bud can't. Give me that gun."

"They aim to get us now," the Reno Kid said as he gave her the gun. "You should've done what King wanted. Like you said, this ain't any of your business. Maybe it ain't too late to make a bargain with 'em."

Guns were blasting outside, lead smashing through the door, screaming in the windows as Nancy Willis answered unsteadily: "Of course we won't."

Blood from his wounded shoulder was wet on the Reno Kid's wrist as he caught her hand and pleaded with her. "It'll get you out of this. I'm done for anyway if they can get me. I'm Slim Considine. This is my land. I'm taking it back from King. They'll gun me down for that. I made a will tonight giving you this land. Don't mix up in my business and lose everything."

"You're wounded," Nancy noticed.

"It ain't much. Keep flat against the wall here. Will you tell Simms out there that you'll go into court like Meeks?"

"No," said Nancy, and she was crying. "You willed your land to me?"

"Jupe Jackson's got the paper."

"Why?"

"I don't know," said the Reno Kid, and his throat grew tight as he realized she was still holding his bloody hand while they crouched against the thick adobe wall. "I'm a liar," he gulped. "I couldn't get you out of my mind. I guess I started loving you when I lit a match out there at Murphy's Well and saw your face."

"I thought Jerry was making it up."

"I told him," said the Reno Kid. "Now will you make a deal with King's men and get out of here safe?"

"Not when it means putting a rope around the neck of someone I love."

"Oh, my God," the Reno Kid gasped. "Say it again."

She was clinging to his hand, and the pain in his swollen left arm didn't matter as he caught her close for a moment. Her lips were there, yielding and sweet, until ricocheting lead screamed across the room and knocked adobe plaster down on them.

"I've *got* to get you outta this," the Reno Kid groaned as he released her.

"Someone's in the back of the house, Slim!" Jerry blurted.

"Stay down close to the wall," the Reno Kid told Nancy. "Never mind using that rifle unless they bust in."

In this house the Reno Kid could move with his eyes closed and know each foot. Beyond that back wall was the kitchen and the small back porch that was built like a shed.

A gush of red flame and black oily smoke filled the kitchen as he jerked open the door. A gun roared at him across the flames. Long Tom Simms had emptied the kerosene can, lighted the fire, and was lingering in the porch doorway for the chance to get Dave Considine's kid brother himself.

The Reno Kid ducked as a bullet drove splinters from the doorway into his cheek. No need to wonder about the end now. This fire couldn't be stopped. The old house would burn fiercely inside the adobe walls, the heavy dirt-covered roof would fall in, the flames would drive them out into the open to be cut down by the waiting guns. Not even Nancy would be spared.

Long Tom Simms had done this—Long Tom Simms, who had gunned Dave down without a chance and cold-bloodedly backed every move of Strickland King.

The Reno Kid was plunging into the fire before he realized what he was doing. The flames licked up about him, the stench of burning oil seared his nostrils, the bucking Colt was slippery inside his bloody hand.

Simms's sleepy eyes had gone wide, the corded neck looked longer, and the tight mouth loose in the leaping red light as the Reno Kid came through the fire. Spurting flame from Simms's gun clubbed the Reno Kid in the side—and then the Kid's gun spun Long Tom Simms half around in the doorway and sprawled him back on the porch. There was light to see the black hole open up between his eyes.

The Kid caught the six-gun from beside Simms's sprawled body and plunged on through the shed porch into the night. Each breath was suddenly a gasping agony, but he could move, could shoot, could still hunt the King gunmen down in the night while they were close around the burning house.

He saw a lurking shadow to the left and went at it with blasting guns. The man wove back into the night, running from the fury that had burst out of the flames. Sobbing for breath, the Reno Kid staggered against the house, reloaded the guns, and lurched on around the end of the house.

"You fellers need help?" a voice called in front of him, and the Reno Kid's spurting guns cut off the words. In ears deafened by the gunfire he heard a shout of alarm. "He kilt Simms an' now he's out gunnin' in the open!"

In front of the house, the Reno Kid lurched with cocked Colts, and realized suddenly that the other guns had gone silent. The wagon teams had bolted away, saddle horses had moved.

North of the house one shot lashed sharply. Another answered. A man yelled: "You got me!"

"Hell, Latigo! I didn't know who you was!"

Lurching toward the voices, the Reno Kid tripped over a

body. Strickland King's body. The rancher hadn't moved after his own man had shot him down.

Well out from the house a man shouted: "King's dead an' Simms is dead! This ain't no fight of mine no more! I'm leavin'!"

The drum of a running horse broke away from the spot.

"Me, too, boys!" A second horse followed a moment later. And then another.

The Reno Kid stood, gasping, and heard them catch horses out there in the night and ride away from a fight that had no profit now that King and his *segundo* were dead and death was loose from the burning house and stalking them in the darkness.

The dancing, crackling flames were gleaming red behind the house when the Reno Kid lurched to the door and called: "I'm coming in, Nancy! They're gone!"

Nancy's arms went about him as he staggered into the doorway. "Slim. What did they do to you? When you went out through that fire, I thought I'd never see you again."

The Reno Kid leaned against the doorway, trying to forget the waves of weakness and the fire in his side as he held her.

"Had to come back and see you once more, anyway," he said huskily. He heard Nancy cry out as his legs buckled—and then there was no more life or sound in the darkness about him.

The clear bright dawn was flooding the sky, smoke was swirling lazily above the gutted house when the Reno Kid heard Nancy say: "Doctor. His eyes are open."

He was lying on a blanket a short distance from the house. Nancy was kneeling by him. Horses and men were there. Coffee was boiling over a fire. Tobe Barrett, the sheriff, and Jupe Jackson were coming from the cook fire.

"You're getting stronger," the young doctor said encouragingly as he felt the Kid's pulse.

The Reno Kid grinned weakly. "Sheriff, I'll be handy for that trial and hanging yet."

"What trial?" Tobe Barrett said.

Jupe Jackson was grinning as he brought a bottle out of his hip pocket.

"Simms is dead," he said. "There isn't any witness against you, young man. Strickland King is dead and no one else has got much interest in seeing you tried for anything. When the doctor told me he couldn't meet Miss Willis's wagon because King's men were bringing him out here to treat a wounded man, I got the sheriff to ride out this way with some men. I had an idea King was up to something. We've got the whole story. If I could get King into court for this, I'd pin him cold. But he's dead and, as your lawyer, I'd say stop worrying and get well."

Nancy was holding the Reno Kid's hand again as she knelt there. "I'll take him home and nurse him there," she told them happily.

"Probably be good for him," the young doctor approved. "He'll need care."

Jerry Willis spoke excitedly at the Reno Kid's head: "Slim, are you really comin' to stay with us?"

The thin youngster was flushed and excited as the Reno Kid turned his head and grinned up from the blanket.

"I'm coming to stay with you . . . and marry Nancy. Think it'll be all right?"

"Gosh." Jerry gulped. His eyes were shining. "It'll be swell. We're gonna have an outlaw in the family! Gosh."

$\star \quad \star \quad \star \quad \star \quad \star$

A GUN FOR THE
RESURRECTION KID

$\star \quad \star \quad \star \quad \star \quad \star$

This story, titled by the author "Gun Pay for Gospel," was completed on January 15, 1938. It was one of the very few Western short stories that T. T. Flynn wrote. For one thing at 2¢ a word, an author didn't make very much money. The author was paid only $70 before commission to his agent. The title was changed to "Gun-Help for the Resurrection Kid" when it appeared in *Star Western* (8/38). Mike Tilden, the editor who originally bought the story, must have liked it, since he chose to reprint it years later as "A Gun for the Resurrection Kid" in *Big-Book Western* (3/54), in the third to last issue of this pulp magazine to be issued by Popular Publications. For its appearance here, while the text of the story has been restored, the title is a variation of that given it by Mike Tilden the two times it was published in Popular Publications Western magazines.

It was sunrise on the Chinango road, and Johnny Starr was dying when he met the Resurrection Kid.

For two hours Johnny had lain huddled in the bushes atop the twenty-foot road bank while the stars paled and the sky turned crimson and gold. His left arm was limp, a raw neck wound still seeped blood, and he gripped a crude leg tourniquet made from a bandanna and a stick. The dripping bandage stained the ground.

The sun bursting over the cañon was warm, but Johnny was cold inside. His breathing was erratic, drowsy. Weakness was coming fast—and still the Chinango road was empty.

Quickly now the hot bright sun would climb up high and Johnny Star would be helpless in the runty bushes, burning with heat and thirst. But whoever passed would never know, because by then he would be too weak to call out.

Eighteen perhaps, no more, Johnny Star looked younger. Tumbled black hair darkened a coffee-tan face, hard and wise as an older man's. Worn chaps, an old jumper, two empty holsters tied low gave him an air of gravity that sat ill with his years.

Johnny looked up, bared his teeth in a hard grin as a black spot soared out of the sun glare.

The buzzards were gathering. They knew. Then the grin vanished as the sound of steel wheel tires came clearly from the road.

171

Holding the tourniquet stick, Johnny struggled up. The two-horse buggy coming on the road held a man and a woman. A bearded rider sided the buggy. Johnny Starr's cry was a husky croak. He lurched up to the bank edge and collapsed dizzily.

Abel Tallow was the bearded rider siding the Resurrection Kid's dusty buggy when the cascade of small stones followed by a rolling body burst down toward the road.

"Hold it, Kid!" Abel caught the bit of the off-horse and helped quiet the frightened team, then galloped to the motionless body. "He's bleeding bad, Doc!"

The Resurrection Kid was already out of the buggy with his black leather bag.

"Wait here, Sue," he told his sister.

One look at Johnny Starr there in the road dust made the Resurrection Kid call: "Sue! The water bottle . . . those towels, and the alcohol." And to Abel Tallow: "Get that waterproof tarp. He's dying. I'll have to work here in the road."

They put Johnny Starr on the tarp in the dust. The Resurrection Kid's fine-lined, smooth young face was set as he worked fast, intently. Sue Jeffry hovered beside him, swiftly carrying out the low-voiced requests.

Abel Tallow inspected his gun and climbed the bank. Blood marked the spot where Johnny Starr had lain. Abel backtracked up the shallow draw beyond, to see what he could see. When he returned, the Resurrection Kid was bandaging swiftly. Johnny Starr was limp, dead-looking on the tarp.

"How's he stack up?" asked Abel Tallow grimly.

The Resurrection Rid shook his head. "I don't know, Abel. I've done the best I can. He's in the hands of a greater Doctor than us all."

Abel Tallow cleared his throat.

"He usually seems to be around to help you, Kid. I backtracked on this *hombre*. He was sheddin' blood all the way."

The Resurrection Kid was red-eyed from lack of sleep, but urgent now. "He shouldn't be moved . . . but we've got to get him into Chinango quickly. Bring up the buggy, Abel. Sue can drive while I hold him."

Johnny Starr wasn't the first helpless stranger the Resurrection Kid and Sue Jeffry had brought to the little log hut on the edge of Chinango.

At first Chinango had laughed, the bellowing careless guffaws of a roaring boom town. Chinango had never seen anything like the pink-cheeked young man who had come in smiling and set up as a doctor and a preacher. He held meetings on the street when he could get someone to listen, and ran with his doctor's bag when anyone needed medicine or sewing up. Never mind the money, Doc Jeffry wouldn't send a bill, didn't want money.

Sue Jeffry played nurse to the percentage girls, the wives who kept off the streets, or helpless gunnies who needed attention. She'd stand out with her brother when he was preaching and keep smiling no matter what was said.

Roaring Bill Hyde, who ran the Hideaway Bar and drank more than most of his customers, gave Doc Jeffry his name in a ribald moment.

"I never seen the beat of it," Roaring Bill announced to a grinning circle at the bar. "Abel Tallow turned down a drink. Says this kid doctor saved him from dyin' after that gunfight at Rocky Ford. To square the debt, Abel promised he'd try Gospel ways. The Kid hooks 'em from the grave an' then doctors their sins. Abel Tallow's Christian ways was dead, clean dead . . . an' the Kid resurrected 'em. He's the Resurrection Kid, or I'm a liar . . . an' if he resurrects you hell-benders and I go busted for lack of customers, I'm still for him. Everybody drink up to the Resurrection Kid."

Roaring Bill Hyde kept his customers. Chinango was too wild, hilarious, and busy to be resurrected. There were mines opening up and talk of a railroad coming through. Chinango had a pick in one hand, a gun in the other, hair on its chest, and a bottle on its hip. A good part of Chinango didn't take to the Resurrection Kid. But the name stuck. The Resurrection Kid was tolerated because he had a lot of friends in the better element.

And out in the hut on the edge of Chinango, Johnny Starr came back from death and found himself being nursed by a soft-speaking young man and a briskly efficient girl. Nobody talked much. Johnny Starr was sick and, later, wary and silent. Johnny had learned to keep his mouth tightly closed.

Outside freight teams and riders went by. A mine stamp mill pounded day and night. Often yells and shots sounded over in Chinango. Johnny Starr's nostrils quivered when he heard sounds of a boom town.

When the girl came in again, Johnny warned harshly: "I ain't got anything to pay for all this. I had some money . . . but I lost it."

Sue Jeffry smiled as she poured medicine into a spoon.

"This isn't costing you anything. Here, take this. What is your name?"

A poker look backed the answer. "Tom Stevens, ma'am."

"Well, Tom, the doctor ordered sleep. I'll close the door, and you close your eyes."

Days later two women called. Johnny heard their voices.

"We'd like the doctor to hold prayer meeting and preach, if he isn't doctoring."

He lay grimly waiting until the women were gone and Sue Jeffry looked in. "Is the doc a preacher?" he demanded violently.

"Yes, but you needn't be afraid of him," Sue Jeffry said.

"Who said I was afraid of anything?"

After she left, he cursed his weakness.

The next afternoon his black eyes were stony and suspicious

when Abel Tallow walked in. Johnny remembered the grizzled beard, the broad-brimmed black hat, leather vest, twin guns, riding low.

"I'm Abel Tallow, son. I've been meanin' to drop in to ask you how you got shot up so."

"Feudin'. They caught up with me."

"I noticed you had two empty gun leathers. Did you get a chance to gun back?"

Johnny Starr's thin face looked trapped, wolfish.

"I wouldn't be here if I had. They shot me outta the saddle. When I got my eyes open, I minded there was a road over to the west an' headed that way."

Abel Tallow pared plug tobacco into his palm. "Wasn't a man in a thousand coulda made it. You was lucky the Resurrection Kid come along after settin' up all night with a dyin' boy."

Johnny gritted his teeth and sat up. He was panting from the effort as he sneered: "What's he doing . . . playin' preacher an' sawbones, too?"

"Don't make sense, does it?" said Abel Tallow calmly. "He trained to be a missionary to the heathen. Had to learn doctorin' and Gospel both. Come time to go, he decided there was enough heathen at his own back door."

"Heathens like me, huh? Preaches how good he is to keep a shot-up stranger around his house, I reckon."

"Nope. He don't talk about what he does, son."

Abel Tallow looked thoughtful when he rode away.

Johnny Starr lay glaring at the ceiling, and then called for pencil and paper to write a letter.

Ten days later he was walking around the cabin, curt, wary, uncommunicative. As he walked, he watched the Resurrection Kid and the girl. Sometimes when hell-raising in Chinango rose high on the night, the Resurrection Kid's finely chiseled young face would look sad. Crashing shots would often send him hurrying out with his doctor's bag.

One night strange riders galloped to the cabin, when the Resurrection Kid was gone. Johnny Starr stopped prowling about the room and listened tensely until a whistle sounded outside. Then he grinned. "Friends of mine, ma'am. I'm leavin'."

Sue Jeffry stood up with quick concern. "You shouldn't try to ride yet."

"I'm tough," said Johnny Starr curtly. "I'm leaving."

Two men were out there in the night, trail-dirty men with belted guns, saddle scabbards holding rifles. They called him Bud, helped him up on an extra horse. From the doorway Sue Jeffry heard her patient growl: "Gimme a pair of guns. Gawd, I been helpless as a baby without 'em."

The spurred horses drummed into the night away from Chinango. Sue Jeffry sighed as she closed the door. Her face was pensive and sad as she went back to her sewing.

Two weeks later Johnny Starr returned.

The Resurrection Kid and his sister were tending flowers before the cabin. Gun-hung, dust-covered, and hard-faced, Starr swaggered to the flower bed. New silver spur chains jingled. His new Stetson was cocked jauntily. His thin face was bold with a hard, sharp humor.

The Resurrection Kid put out his hand. "Well, Johnny, how's the leg?"

"Still limpin' some, Doc. Howdy, ma'am. Surprised to see me back?"

Sue Jeffry laughed and pushed back her sunbonnet. "You said you'd be back."

"Didn't believe that, did you?"

"I always believe what I'm told."

"You'll learn better," Johnny Starr told her. "Here, Doc . . . I got this soon as I could. Two hundred gold in this stack. I'll double it if you say the word."

"There's no charge, Johnny."

"Take it. I'm trying to settle fair an' square."

"There's nothing to settle, Johnny."

"If you don't want money, what do you want?"

The Resurrection Kid smiled faintly. "I could use your soul, Johnny."

"Preachin', huh?"

The Resurrection Kid laughed. "No, Johnny. You asked me."

"I'll stick to my guns. You Gospel talkers don't know what it's all about. Last chance on the *dinero*. You want it?"

"No," said the Resurrection Kid, smiling.

Johnny was scowling as he headed into Chinango with the other riders. "I don't savvy that Gospel hound."

"You worry about it, Bud," said the older rider on the left, grinning. "Here's Chinango . . . and I'm gonna chaw hard before we swaller it."

Abel Tallow was trail-weary at sundown when he stopped at the cabin.

"So he's back," said Abel, frowning. "How many was with him, Doc? Only two? You sure?"

Grimly Abel Tallow rode on into Chinango. And in the next three hours Abel grew grimmer.

Chinango's Saturday nights were wild. Ranch wagons, freight wagons, buggies, and saddle horses cluttered the rutted, dusty street. Booted miners with Saturday pay, prospectors, cowmen, land sharks, gold buyers, gamblers, strangers were all in the crowd. Stores were open, the bank was busy, saloons, gambling spots seethed with trade.

Johnny Starr moved through the thick of it, with a hard wild swagger for those who flocked around his reckless spending.

In the Hideaway Bar Abel Tallow heard a bearded miner call: "Ain't you the young feller that was sick up at the Resurrection Kid's cabin?"

Johnny Starr turned quickly. "What's it to you?"

Abel Tallow trailed behind when Johnny Starr swaggered out and ran across the Resurrection Kid, preaching before the corner bank. A smoky kerosene flare lighted the doctor's smooth earnest face and the humor of the listeners.

Johnny Starr sneered and walked around the corner. Tallow caught up with him in the darker shadows fronting a vacant lot. "Turn off here, Starr."

Johnny Starr obeyed the prodding gun. "So you know about me. You an' the doc are in cahoots for the reward, I reckon."

"I'll talk," said Abel Tallow. "The day we found you, I backtracked your trail. You was shot at a campfire quarreling over stolen money. A Wells, Fargo money sack was still smokin' in the ashes. There was a Wells, Fargo hold-up over on the Dagger Basin trail four days before. While you was in bed, the marshal's office got a circular about it. A thousand dollars reward on each of the two rannies who did it. Keep them hands up. I'll take your guns."

Some of the swagger was gone, now, but Johnny Starr could jeer. "So you and the preacher are makin' five hundred apiece on me. I savvy now, plenty, why he turned down my money."

"Keep walkin' . . . straight ahead up the slope there beyond town," ordered Abel Tallow grimly. "You're worth more'n a thousand now. Two days ago I was in Forktown when eight killers went hog-wild at the bank an' killed two people before they got away with the money. They was all masked, but I spotted your limp when you run outta the bank. I knowed then you shoulda been hung long ago. Three of you rode in together today. I've seen you meeting the others on the sly around town. You're all set for some dirty work here in Chinango. And the

178

Resurrection Kid who saved your life is down there on the street preaching without any idea what's due to bust loose."

Johnny Starr was venomous. "Maybe he's waitin' to collect his share of the law money. He worked hard enough for it."

"His work was savin' your no-good young life. I shouldn't have listened to him when he told me to burn that Reward circular an' let the good in you come out after you got well. All you done was bring back blood money from that Forktown hold-up."

"That's all I had. I always settle what I owe, mister. Nobody ever said Johnny Starr rode off without paying up."

The logged-off slope now was covered with old stumps, dead branches. Abel Tallow gripped his prisoner's collar as they walked ahead. "This is one bill you can't settle. You can't buy Gospel work. He found you dying an' brought you to his bed . . . and it didn't mean enough to even keep you away from Chinango with your wolf tricks. Plenty don't like the doc's ways. If they find he turned a killer loose to raid Chinango, it'll be the end of the Kid."

"Why didn't he tell me?"

"A gun and a noose is all your kind can understand."

"You're a liar. Lock me up and give him the reward money, if it'll square my bill."

Abel Tallow swore. "I can't even have you locked up. The story'll get out about the Forktown killings, which'll be blamed on the doc. All I can do is gun-whip you half dead here in the night and send you back to tell those other killers to get out of town."

Johnny Starr stopped and looked down the slope toward the town lights. "That won't help you, mister. Last year I warned part of this bunch away from a bank . . . an' went back later and got it all myself. They'd think I was tryin' it again. I'm only with 'em now because I'm man enough to back up anything they try. Soon as I get in their way, they'll go for me. A crowd with guns is the only thing that'll hold 'em back tonight . . . an' it better be quick. They're gathering now to raid the bank right where the doc's preachin'. Gimme my guns."

Abel Tallow cried: "Hold still, you young fool!"

Abel had been sure no one would be fool enough to try it. Johnny Starr's hand was knocking the gun away just as Abel pulled the trigger.

The blast struck Johnny's side, and his wiry figure whirling fast, knocked the gun away. His other hand caught a gun from Abel's belt and clubbed Abel sprawling. Johnny snatched back his own guns and gasped: "If Gospel work takes Gospel pay, I'll try it."

He was hit, hit hard. He ran down the slope with awkward, lurching strides, one hand holding his side. Abel Tallow staggered up, held his head for a moment, and followed him.

By his smoky flare, the Resurrection Kid was preaching to an audience that shifted and changed as men paused and moved on.

Nobody noticed the riders moving to the bank corner from three directions. Seven of them coming to the bank and dismounting.

Johnny Starr was noticed first—a thin, wiry, gasping figure that burst out on the corner with drunken steps, looked around with bloodshot eyes, and then yelled: "Run, Doc, it's a hold-up!"

A dozen men saw Johnny Starr lurch toward the hitch rack where the strange riders were dismounting, heard him call: "Ride on! I'm takin' over the town tonight!"

Two dozen men heard the angry yell in front of the hitch rack: "Get the double-crossin' little snake!"

Not many saw it all, saw Johnny Starr stop and set himself against the bullets, his two guns roaring, saw Abel Tallow dash around the corner and begin shooting. Men at the hitch rack leaped for their horses and spurred away. There had been four of them—and three were left as Johnny Starr dropped his empty smoking guns and fell.

The Resurrection Kid had his bag there a step behind Abel Tallow. But the bag remained closed. Any man could see that Johnny Starr was through. The first few who rushed up were the only ones to hear Johnny Starr gasp to the Resurrection Kid kneeling over him: "You think we're square now, Doc?"

"Of course, Johnny. Take it easy, boy."

"Gimme your hand, Doc . . . it's dark. I didn't savvy your Gospel ways, but I always aim to pay. . . ."

A hundred men heard what Johnny Starr had said. It didn't make much sense.

Roaring Bill Hyde came as close as anyone as he served free drinks across the bar. "I never seen the beat. A tough little gun artist like him. The doc helped him once . . . and he died talkin' Gospel. Drink up, men. Drink to Johnny Starr, who saved the bank . . . an' to the doc, who resurrected Johnny Starr."

ABOUT THE AUTHOR

T. T. Flynn was born Thomas Theodore Flynn, Jr., in Indianapolis, Indiana. He was the author of over a hundred Western stories for such leading pulp magazines as Street & Smith's *Western Story Magazine,* Popular Publications' *Dime Western,* and Dell's *Zane Grey's Western Magazine.* He lived much of his life in New Mexico and spent much of his time on the road, exploring the vast terrain of the American West. His descriptions of the land are always detailed, but he used them not only for local color but also to reflect the heightening of emotional distress among the characters within a story. Following the Second World War, Flynn turned his attention to the book-length Western novel and in this form also produced work that has proven imperishable. Five of these novels first appeared as original paperbacks, most notably *The Man from Laramie* (1954) which was also featured as a serial in *The Saturday Evening Post* and subsequently made into a memorable motion picture directed by Anthony Mann and starring James Stewart, and *Two Faces West* (1954) which deals with the problems of identity and reality and served as the basis for a television series. He was highly innovative and inventive and in later novels, such as *Night of the Comanche Moon* (Five Star Westerns, 1995), concentrated on deeper psychological issues as the source for conflict, rather than more elemental motives like greed. Flynn is at his best in stories that combine mystery—not surprisingly, he also wrote detective fiction—with suspense and action in an artful balance. The psychological dimensions of Flynn's Western fiction came increasingly to encompass a confrontation with ethical principles about how one must live, the values that one must hold dear above all else, and his belief that there must be a balance in all things. The cosmic meaning of the mortality of all living creatures had become for him a unifying metaphor for the fragility and dignity of life itself. *Cantrell* will be his next **Five Star Western.**